# FIRSTBORN ACADEMY

## SHADOW TRIALS

ISLA FROST

Copyright © 2019 by Isla Frost
All rights reserved.

Published by JFP Trust
2019 First Print Edition

ISBN: 978 0 6482532 6 6

www.islafrost.com

# CHAPTER 1

I stroked Mila's chubby cheek, her skin damp with tears, and held my handkerchief to her nose before a snot bubble could erupt.

"Blow," I ordered.

She did.

Heaven help me if even this was a memory I might cherish. A mundane and kind of gross aspect of family life that I was somehow loath to miss out on.

I grinned at her. "That was a wet one."

My voice wobbled on the words, but I hoped she wouldn't notice as I tucked the handkerchief into her breast pocket. "You can keep it."

Over the years, I'd given her more of my handkerchiefs than I could count. It always amazed me that in a world where dirt was a rare commodity, my little sister was always covered in it.

The thought made me spare a glance for the cityscape below.

Even from our rooftop vantage point, cityscape was a generous term for the concrete wasteland that had once been Los Angeles. The power had long ago been cut off, taking most of mankind's modern conveniences with it, and signs of disrepair were everywhere. Buckled tarmac, half-toppled buildings, broken glass. Even the once-bright colors had conceded defeat, fading like bones bleached by the sun into a uniform drab gray. Though a few washed-out billboards still promoted obsolete products from the Before if you peered closely enough.

But some of the city had remained intact in the years since the takeover. And until today, one of those intact buildings had been my home.

Not anymore.

But it wasn't the building that hurt so much to leave behind.

Reuben, my younger brother, was scuffing his foot against the ground like he didn't care. But his red-rimmed eyes and tight-knuckled fists told a different story. I ruffled his hair in the way he'd come to hate in the past few months and pulled him close.

"Look after everyone for me, okay, squirt? And don't worry about me. You'll have your hands full keeping Mila out of trouble and Dad out of the dessert rations."

His mouth tugged upward at one corner, and he shoved me away. Gently though. His fingers gripping the fabric of my shirt a moment too long before releasing. A subconscious gesture that made my chest ache.

My mother. Her eyes were on my face, but I sensed she didn't really see it. She had looked right through me ever since I could remember. A distance that only grew as I did. A distance she'd created to prevent her heart from breaking in this inevitable moment, my dad said. One I'd resented until now. Until it didn't hurt so much to say goodbye to her.

I hugged her stiffly but softly in a moment of understanding and turned to my father.

Dad. His eyes were shining with wet. He had never held me at arm's length, never put distance between us. Instead, it was if he'd tried to pour all the love he held for my lifetime into these past seventeen years. I was his favorite. He told me so all the time.

Then again, I'd overheard him telling both Mila and Reuben that a bunch of times too.

I embraced him. "I love you."

The words left me in a whisper. Not because it was anything other than complete truth, but because my throat was so tight I could barely squeeze the sound out.

"I love you to the stars and back, Nova." His voice was as constricted as my own as he spoke the familiar endearment. A play on my name that belonged to just us alone. "Please come back to us. If you possibly can."

His huge arms wrapped around me in the strong and tender shelter he'd offered since I was an infant.

A shelter I would never experience again.

3

I swiped at my eyes, angry with myself. I had promised myself I would not cry. That I would wait until I was through the runegate to fall apart.

The guilt my family would live with was burden enough without me adding to it in this moment.

The people left behind paid too. In their own way. I'd seen it time and time again. Mrs. Crocus, who didn't smile anymore since giving up her daughter six years ago. Her remaining son, who bore the strain of knowing he wasn't enough to ease her grief. The Hernandez family, whose home had grown quiet now without Gloria's contagious laughter.

I'd always known the cost. Known too that there was no other option.

Thirty years ago the Blythe family broke the Agreement, refusing to send their firstborn. An entire bloodline, three generations, had been wiped out in the blink of an eye.

So I forced my chest—my chest, which felt like it was on the point of collapsing—out in a deep breath, lifted my chin, and stepped out of my father's arms for the very last time.

"I love you all," I told them, meeting each of their eyes and attempting to etch every detail of their faces to memory. "Live well. Don't let grief get in the way of that. And enjoy the extra serving of fruitcake."

The rest went unsaid. Make my sacrifice worthwhile. Love and laugh often. No matter what my future held, I wanted the very best for them.

I did not wait for their replies. I couldn't. I needed to go while my legs would still obey me.

So I turned and stepped up to the waiting runegate.

# CHAPTER 2

Whatever I faced, I would not face it alone. Ameline, my best friend since forever, was going with me. Our birthdays were but days apart. And now she was standing beside me before the ominous, glowing runegate, her hand in mine.

That fact gave me the strength I needed to take the final step.

My vision went black, like the snuffing out of a lantern on a moonless night. For a split second I feared I'd gone blind. Then my skin prickled as if a thousand ants were crawling up my legs, down my neck, and over my face. I could barely feel Ameline's hand over the sensation, but that only made me hang on more stubbornly. I heard something. A whimper? But the sound was muted like I was underwater, and then my ears popped, the prickling sensation ceased as quickly as it came, and I could see again.

I checked to make sure that Ameline was still beside me, and something in my chest loosened at the sight of her pale face. Never mind it was rigid with fear. We were together. Until the end.

The first thing I noticed was the gloom. We'd left our home on a crisp but sunlit autumn day and now stood in a dimly lit place heavy with shadows. Despite my warm scarf and warmer coat, a chill crept over me.

We were in some sort of tall, narrow room. A tower maybe? And the very walls felt alive.

I scanned our surroundings. Noticed the weak circle of sunlight from a window high above. Too high to escape through. Noticed the threadbare rug offering little insulation from the cold and ancient timber floor. And the sparse furnishings, beautiful but worn, left over from another time. Before the world went to hell.

Did the strange creatures depicted on the wallpaper just move?

Ameline's hand tightened around my own.

I took a deep breath. And another. There was enough to fear here without letting my imagination get the better of me.

There was no sign of the runegate we'd come through. No way back. So I shuffled forward a single step, drawing Ameline with me.

"Hello?" I called. "We've arrived from Los Angeles to honor the Firstborn Agreement."

No answer.

No sound at all except for our unsteady breathing.

Which was when I noticed what was missing. No clock on the wall. No fire crackling in the hearth. Nothing but this antique furniture. And…

I gulped.

No door.

My heart sped up, and my gaze flew to that window again. So high above. Three stories maybe. And nothing on the wall but the strange wallpaper that seemed to move in my peripheral vision. Certainly nothing to grip.

Was this a test of some kind?

It must be.

Surely firstborns were not simply sent here to die. To starve slowly in this small, timeworn room. There would be bones if that were the case. So many bones.

Unless they were eaten afterward.

No one had seen the creatures we were now bound to.

We did not know if they were the ones that called themselves world walkers. The race that led the invasion who'd looked almost human yet possessed powers that were anything but. Or whether our Agreement was with one of the countless strange beings that had come with them. Creatures of legend. Dragons. Unicorns. Griffins and more. Or if, worst of all, our future now belonged to the monstrous, devouring darkness that had wiped out life from Europe before the last satellites failed.

In truth, we rarely saw *any* other species—those that did tended not to survive the encounter. Nothing but strange flickers of movement in the forests that surrounded the safety of our concrete jungle, so often out of the corner of your eye where you couldn't be sure if you'd seen anything more than your own fears.

But if our "benefactors" were so fast, so impossible for us to protect ourselves against, and so hungry for our flesh, why would they sign the Agreement to begin with?

Food and basic provisions showed up on the first day of each month, enough to supply the colony's needs until the next delivery was due.

As a twelve-year-old, I'd snuck out to watch, hiding in the wrecked body of an old car to learn who it was that brought our rations. I'd stayed up all night, shivering in the cold. But the delivery hadn't come. Nor did it come the next night, or the next. Not until I'd given up and returned home to the refuge of my blankets had our precious provisions been delivered. Four days late.

I'd never tried again.

And "all" these unknown beings had required in return for their protection from the forest trying to reclaim our city and the monthly provisions that kept us from starving—was the firstborn of every family to be surrendered to them at the age of seventeen.

Were we... livestock to them? It was a suspicion I'd never voiced aloud but one I couldn't shake either. Whoever they were, they fed us and kept us safe and took no more from the "herd" than could be spared without unduly shrinking our population.

An arrangement that sounded an awful lot like what grandmother had told me of her parents' cattle ranch in the Before.

The familiar thoughts were not helpful in this creepy little room.

A sound at our backs made me whirl. A buzzing of energy and something scuffing the floorboards.

Not something. A girl. She stumbled forward and stopped. Her wide, dark eyes flying around the room before landing on us.

She straightened to her full height, which was decidedly underwhelming, and gave us an appraising once-over.

"So... do you come here often?"

I stared.

She grinned, the expression quick and sharp across her heart-shaped face. "I'm Bryn. Did you just arrive too?"

"Yes," I confirmed faintly, still wondering if she knew something I didn't. "I'm Nova, and this is Ameline."

"It's a pleasure, I'm sure."

The girl brushed past us, breaking my and Ameline's unspoken agreement to huddle together, frozen in place. She helped herself to the single chair in the room, clonked her heavy boots onto the ornate desk beside it, and folded her arms.

"So what's the situation here? Are there more of us

coming? Have you met our new overlords or whatever yet?"

Ameline was stiff beside me. She was not a rule breaker by nature. In fact, she was the furthest thing from a natural rule breaker I'd ever known, and I knew what she was thinking.

"Um," she said, "are you sure you shouldn't be more respectful of the furniture? *They* might not like it."

The new girl, Bryn, shrugged. "I'm sure the oh-so-powerful ones can handle feet on furniture. Besides, who's watching?"

Her question made my skin crawl. *Were* they watching?

"They could be observing us," I pointed out, giving Ameline's hand a squeeze. "We only arrived a minute ago, but there's no door out of here, and no one answered when we announced ourselves. I wondered if it might be a test of some kind."

Ameline's brow furrowed. "Or maybe they're just busy."

Bryn grinned again. "So they're either too busy to greet the human sacrifices they demanded, or they're testing us. In either case, sounds to me like we should find our own way out of here."

She swung her feet off the desk—much to Ameline's relief—and started tapping the wall with her fist. Listening for a hollow noise that might indicate a secret passage, I guessed.

Her reasoning made sense enough to me. Plus there could be no harm in looking, could there?

My question was impossible to answer. We knew nothing about our new masters. But I was sick of standing around feeling helpless, so I gave Ameline's hand a last squeeze and joined Bryn in testing the walls.

We made it around the room in a few minutes. One section sounded different from the rest, but I could find no seam or gap that would indicate a hidden door. Ameline joined us and traced her fingers over the wallpaper on the off chance something would trigger it to open. Bryn did the same but with a lot more force behind her fingers.

Nothing happened.

"Maybe something else in the room could be the trigger mechanism?" Ameline suggested hesitantly.

I was proud of her for participating in the search and glad for Bryn's influence. It was hard to remain terrified when the girl was banging around the room like it was some sort of grand adventure. And she'd been right in at least one thing: doing something was better than nothing.

The three of us split up to inspect and shift every object we could find. In a moment of inspiration, I pulled back the rug. But only more ancient floorboards and a light layer of dirt hid beneath. Damn.

Half an hour passed, and we were no closer to finding an exit.

Which was when Bryn withdrew a switchblade and plunged it into the wall.

Ameline, who'd been sizing up the chair and whether she was allowed to sit in it, flinched. "What are you doing?"

Bryn wiggled the knife free, then plunged it into the wall again.

"Looks like the window is the only exit. And since there's not enough furniture in here to stack and climb, I'm testing if we can make toeholds."

She seesawed the blade until a chunk of plaster and wood came free, then inspected the hole she'd created with self-satisfaction.

I was unsure whether to get out my own dagger and help. It was strapped discreetly to my thigh, and I'd wanted to keep it hidden. To have an element of surprise in an emergency.

Although I had no idea what to expect from the beings we were now bound to, I did have a plan. I would keep my head down and do whatever it took to survive while I gleaned as much information as possible.

Until I'd learned enough to carry out my secret agenda.

It was a secret I'd never shared with anyone. Not even Ameline. A secret I'd been working toward my whole life.

But in all the scenarios I'd imagined befalling us after stepping through the runegate, being stuck inside a room without even glimpsing those responsible was not one of them. So after another moment of hesitation, I slipped my dagger from its sheath and went to help Bryn.

Besides, I really wanted to see what was outside that window.

Any advantage, any glimpse, any knowledge of what we'd been brought here for could give us some small edge. Maybe one that would save our lives.

Behind us, Ameline sighed and sank into the chair.

As soon as the first hole was large enough for a toehold, Bryn tested it with her weight. "Good. Looks like this'll work. Help me drag the desk over here, will you?"

We positioned it beneath the window, climbed on top, and started the next hole a lot higher up.

"Where are you from?" I asked Bryn as we worked.

"In what remains of Austin, Texas, I was told. Which isn't much."

"Were there no other seventeen-year-old firstborns this year?"

I felt bad for her. For entering this place alone. But she seemed unbothered by it.

"Nope. But I'm glad enough to leave. My mom died in childbirth, and my dad was a mean drunk. I figure whatever's here can't be much worse." She dug out more shards of plaster and wood, then stabbed the wall again, hard. "Or if it is, at least I'll get to have seen something other than one disintegrating city before I die. Not many people can say that these days."

The holes we were carving were farther up now, and we had to take turns. Using our existing toe and hand-holds, we'd climb the wall and dig the next one out above our heads while the excavated material pelted our faces. It was awkward and difficult work, dangerous too the higher we got, and we were both covered in dust and wood splinters. But at least the wallpaper creatures around our blades had ceased seeming to move.

Bryn had the luck to carve the final hole. I stamped down my desire to be first. It had been Bryn's plan after all. I could wait another minute.

She sheathed her blade, shook the bigger chunks of debris out of her short black hair, and scrambled upward until she gripped the window ledge.

"Oh hell no," she whispered.

"What? What is it?" Worry and curiosity made my fingers itch to clamber up beside her.

Bryn didn't answer for several long seconds. Just stared out through the glass. Then she said, "You should see for yourself," and began the climb down, her motions slower than on the way up.

Impatient now, I shoved my toes into the first hole the moment she dropped to the desk. Anticipation thrummed in my chest as I climbed, forcing myself to be careful, to check each foothold and hand purchase, until at last my fingers brushed the window ledge.

"What in the devil's fiddlesticks is going on in here?"

The question had not come from Ameline or Bryn. The voice was deep and rumbly with an edge of rust.

Like when Mila drove her wooden toy truck over the wreckage of a real one.

I whirled and almost lost my grip.

A door that definitely hadn't been there earlier had opened on the far wall, and standing in the doorway was...

Well, I had no idea *what* it was.

# CHAPTER 3

The creature was as large as a man and stood upright on a powerful set of legs. But there the resemblance ended.

It had *two* heads mounted next to each other— nearly identical with long, tapered snouts, large dark eyes, and small rounded ears. Black fur coated the underside of the jaws and delicate noses while the topside was coated in scales.

The scales thickened and grew into large armored plates as they descended over the creature's head, down its back, and along the heavy tail that hung to the floor and extended another five feet. More of the black fur coated its belly, and a combination of both sheathed the forelimbs right up to the long clawed fingers.

One of the two heads was muttering something to the other, too quiet for us to catch.

The second was staring at me.

The sight of it made my own limbs—so normal by

comparison—tremble. Or maybe that was because I was still clinging to the wall three stories above the ground.

Not that the creature looked *scary* per se. It would've been cute if it'd been a fraction of the size and the claws couldn't have ripped me open in one quick slash.

But claws or no claws, I was damned if I was going to climb down until I'd seen out the window.

My fingers curled around the sill, and my foot found the last toehold. I turned my back on the creature and pulled myself up the last few feet. Only to see an external window shutter slam shut.

"What the?"

Frustration spiked through me, but what was I going to do? Break the window and wrestle with the apparently magical shutter?

I swiveled back to the creature, who was still staring —or was that glaring?—in my direction.

Had *it* been responsible for the shutter?

I fought my urge to glare back.

Ameline stepped forward on my behalf. She might be shy around human strangers, but she'd always been fearless around animals. Anything from feral cats to the cockatrice that had found its way into one of the few remaining human-controlled gardens when I was six. The garden that I'd happened to be playing in.

Ameline had saved me then, and she was doubtless trying to save me now too.

She waited till the creature's heads had trained on her movement and then bowed.

"Apologies if we've wronged you. We thought this doorless room"—she hesitated since the beast thing was clearly standing in a doorway—"well, you see, it did *seem* doorless a few minutes ago. Um, anyway, we thought it might be some sort of test."

I spared the window a final glance before scrambling down to stand beside my friend.

"Test?" asked the head on the right. "You hear that, Glennys? I *told* you we couldn't trust them to be left alone in here. But you just *insisted* we clean up that mess first. And now they've gone and destroyed the wall and frightened the wallpaper too. Look at the poor creatures, terrified half to death!"

"Oh, don't be so dramatic, Glenn," said the head on the left.

The voice was higher and softer and sounded exasperated. "That one apologized, didn't she? And the wall will heal in time, and it'll be like they were never here. It's not nearly as bad as if we'd left that manticore cub prowling around the dining hall or the megalith moth in the linen cupboard. Now quiet down; you're scaring the humans."

They stopped arguing momentarily, and Ameline took advantage of the brief respite.

"Are you the ones we've come to honor our Agreement with?"

The head on the right extended its snout to the ceiling and let out a harsh braying sound. Even Bryn flinched.

"Stop laughing at them," admonished the head on the left. Glennys, I thought the other had called it. But it—she?—was making a quiet huffing noise as if trying not to laugh herself.

"It *is* funny though, I have to admit. No, firstborns, we are merely the custodian here. You will meet the ones you are bound to soon enough. Tomorrow in fact."

"Oh," Ameline said. "What's your relationship with them then, if I may be so bold?"

The head on the right, which had mercifully finished laughing, considered Ameline. Was that a softening in those large dark eyes?

"That one does have nice manners, I'll give you that. We were rescued by a w—"

Glennys headbutted him.

"Ahem. We were rescued by them many, many years ago and brought along when they traveled here. We're the only one of our kind on this planet."

"Rescued?" Ameline asked. "Does that mean they're, well, nice?"

Glenn did that braying laugh thing again. Glennys sighed.

"Ignore him, child. He says *one of a kind* like we're some kind of art exhibit rather than glorified pets. Now come along, and we'll show you to your rooms."

She'd evaded Ameline's question about their *rescuers* being nice. But rooms sounded hopeful. Better than the dungeon or slaughterhouse anyway. The strange creature was already sweeping from the room, tail dragging behind it.

Ameline tucked her arm through mine and whispered, "They're like a black-bellied pangolin—except much, much larger and with two heads."

She seemed to think that would mean something to me, but I'd never heard of a pangolin.

We followed like obedient children, stepping into a grand hallway that, while not as lofty as the tower room, was still a good two stories tall. Rich wood paneling reached as high as my elbow, with more strange wallpaper above that. Above us, an ornate ceiling featured a three-dimensional, swirling pattern embellished in gold.

So much color, so much *care* given to details that served no functional purpose felt foreign to me. Yet beyond Glenn and Glennys and the possibly moving wallpaper, there was nothing to suggest this was anything but a grand old manor, built by humans a few hundred years ago and maintained ever since.

I'd seen pictures of houses like these. There were even a few like it in Los Angeles, though they'd been built later and poorly maintained since the takeover.

This one wasn't in perfect condition, but nothing was broken, the timber gleamed with a fresh coat of oil, and there wasn't a speck of dust in sight. So who on earth did this place belong to?

Maybe we could learn more from the creature we were following. If I could recover from our rocky start.

"Um, sorry again about the wallpaper," I said.

Bryn winked at me, then raised her voice. "I would be too if I'd had anything to do with it."

I smirked. Her black hair was caked with pale gray plaster dust, and I was pretty sure Glenn and Glennys were intelligent enough to connect the dots.

I tugged a strand of my own dark brown hair, which was no doubt equally filthy. "You might want to look in a mirror before you try that one on."

Bryn did a double take, her hand rising in belated realization.

Ameline giggled. Bryn and I joined in. And then, because the creature walked surprisingly fast, we hurried to catch up.

"Watch the tail!" the gruff one barked.

I was glad their voices were distinct, because being behind them meant I had to reorient myself on which was which.

"Oh really," Glennys scolded. "I'm sure they're perfectly capable of watching where they're going."

"You thought they'd be perfectly capable of sitting in a room unattended for an hour without damaging it too, and look how that turned out."

One of the heads, Glennys I thought it was, turned and mouthed the word *sorry.*

"You know I don't like it when you talk behind our back," muttered the other one, but they kept walking, and none of us trod on their tail.

Ameline caught onto my desire to obtain information and formally introduced us. Conversation flowed more freely after that. And as we gawked at the changing decoration and trailed up a creaking stairway, we soaked in what they were willing to tell us. Glenn and Glennys were from a race of beings called the golin who quite literally became one when they chose lifelong mates. Their masters, and the ones that we were now bound to, had rescued them and then magically gifted them with a longer lifespan and the ability to speak multiple languages.

"Be careful about accepting gifts from them," Glenn had grumbled. "Now I'm stuck with Glennys for ten lifetimes, and she never stops talking."

Ameline, hurrying to head off another bout of bickering, asked, "What did you need rescuing from?"

"Our own kind," Glennys replied heavily. "We had a difference of beliefs."

"Oh." Ameline fell silent, not wanting to blunder into sensitive territory.

Bryn had no such qualms. "What difference of beliefs was that?"

"They believed we should die," Glennys said.

"And we didn't," Glenn finished.

I felt my eyebrows rise unwillingly and fought them down as the creature, or couple, or golin halted and touched a section of wall. The figures on the wallpaper darted to one side—*definitely* moving—and a door materialized before our eyes.

"Here's your room then."

I hesitated, not sure I wanted to be trapped in

another room. "Um, will we be locked in again?"

"What do you mean?" asked Glennys.

"Is the door going to stay when you leave?"

Glenn sniffed. "Of course it will. We don't create doors out of thin air, you know."

Funny, as it seemed to me they'd done just that.

"But you do need permission to open it," Glennys added.

Which sounded like the essence of a lock as well.

The golin pointed at a coiled serpent on the wallpaper. Its scales glinted a dark ruby red, and it raised its head when the golin's claws drew near. All the better to see its oversized fangs.

"Just touch your finger here so it can taste you. Then Millicent will know this dormitory is yours and will let you inside. Now, do you want to room together?"

"Yes," Ameline said at the same time as Bryn shrugged.

"Why not?"

"Who's Millicent?" I asked, peering more closely at the red serpent before touching my finger to it. "Ouch!"

Something on the wall stabbed me hard enough to draw blood. Quite a lot of blood. It welled from my fingertip and dripped onto the floor. Where it promptly disappeared into the timber.

"Pfft," Glenn said, opening the door. "You can hardly feel it. That's just Millicent identifying you. Can't be too careful with shapeshifting and all that, but you can't change your blood."

Well, most of my reaction had been shock, but I thought *hardly feel it* was a stretch. Whatever the hell had punctured my skin had done it with enough force to bruise.

"Do we have to do that every time we go in and out of our room?"

And did we need to be worried about shapeshifting beings trying to trick their way inside?

"Just in," Glennys assured me.

I regarded my throbbing digit and hoped whatever we'd been brought here to do didn't require fine finger work.

Bryn glanced at me and offered her own hand to the serpent. I saw her flinch, but forewarned, she didn't react any more than that.

Ameline stepped forward too, more hesitant. She did not like pain. Or blood. But we'd imagined this day would hold far worse horrors, so she pressed her finger to the wallpaper too.

No flinch. Huh.

"It barely hurt," she whispered uncertainly. "Maybe I didn't do it right?"

The golin had already entered our new room and was bustling around seemingly ensuring everything was in order. But Glennys glanced back to see what was taking us so long and spotted Bryn and me bleeding onto the floor.

"Oh," she said while Glenn checked the woodpile by the fireplace. "I see what's going on now. Millicent must be upset at you two for harming her wall. So she took a little bit of *extra* blood for compensation."

That would explain why it hadn't hurt Ameline. Sort of.

Bryn glowered at her mangled finger. "Who the hell is Millicent?"

The golin waved its claws vaguely around the room. "Millicent Manor. Didn't we tell you?"

My jaw dropped as the implication sank in.

"The building is… alive?" asked Ameline.

"Don't call her a building; she doesn't like that. Too impersonal. Stick to Millicent. Or the manor. Or home. That one she loves most of all." Glennys said this like it made perfect sense and bared her teeth in what might've been a smile. "Now then, we've tarried long enough. Settle yourselves in and then go to the dining hall when you get hungry. We'd best greet the next lot of new students."

Glenn shot me a meaningful look. "Before they do any *more* damage."

The torrent of bewildering information made my next question a fraction too slow. "Wait, what do you mean *students*?"

But the golin waddled off without explanation— either failing to hear me or pretending to. And Ameline, Bryn, and I were left alone in a strange room all over again.

A living and apparently *angry* room.

And we had no idea how to find the dining hall.

# CHAPTER 4

The room we'd paid with our blood to gain access to was technically single story, but the decorative, sculpted ceiling sloped upward with the pitch of the roof, giving it the same spacious feel as the rest of the manor. Albeit a little less grand.

There were three beds along the right wall, each with a wooden trunk at the foot, and on the left, three padded armchairs were positioned around the ornate but functional fireplace.

The wood paneling in the hall gave way to yet more wallpaper in here. Lucky us. But more disconcerting than the possibly sentient creatures that would watch us while we slept was the large arched window on the far wall.

On the up side, it no longer mattered that I'd been prevented from peering out the other window. I could see more than any person in their right mind would want to out of this one.

Plenty of the buildings back in Los Angeles had windows, of course. It was the greenery directly beyond the glass panes that was so daunting.

A sea of swirling mist, reaching trunks, and tangled foliage fought for space among the thick carpet of decaying leaves that made up the forest floor. All sorts of monsters could hide in a place like that.

Huge intimidating trees dwarfed the manor, even up here on the top floor. Few of them bothered to display the traditional colors of autumn, their dense canopy blocking out the overcast sky and with it any hope of guessing at our location.

And if that wasn't bad enough, vicious-looking vines with blood-red thorns the length of my fingers climbed up the manor itself, the tenacious tendrils clinging to the window frame like it was trying to get in.

No wonder Bryn had cursed when she'd looked through that other window.

In the ruined city I'd grown up in, only the fool-hardy or insane lived on the edge of the forest.

Nature—or the magical thing it had morphed into since the invasion—was dangerous.

Sleeping near it invited a carnivorous tree to snatch you from your bed and bury you alive to nourish its roots. Or a wandering monster to smash through your window for a fast-food snack. Or any one of a hundred nightmare scenarios humans from the Before could only dream of.

So scenic views had become ominous landscapes, something we'd been warned away from since birth.

Yet despite the danger and the fear that came with it, the greenery had always called to me. It was beautiful. Far more beautiful than any concrete vista could ever be. And that beauty drew my gaze even when I knew better.

It dared me to enter. To explore.

To die.

Perhaps it was just instinct left over from when greenery meant food, water, life—instinct not yet erased by evolution.

I wasn't foolish enough to *follow* the pull. But with the glass offering a thin veneer of safety, I found myself stepping closer.

To see more.

Past the wicked thorny vine and before the edge of the forest stretched a manicured green lawn. Something I'd only ever seen in old photos. Equally manicured garden beds and a lake too perfectly round to be natural disrupted the clipped grass in geometric lines.

But far more bizarre than any of that were the twelve-foot topiary hedge cats that lined the edge of the manor grounds. Spaced at regular intervals, they sat on their leafy-green haunches and stared outward into the forest. As if they knew what lurked within. As if they were the guardians of this strange place.

My gaze was drawn along with theirs into the shadowy depths, and goose bumps prickled along my skin. I backed away from the window.

This sentient manor probably *did* have some kind of protection the city lacked. It was senseless for the beings behind the Agreement to go to so much trouble keeping humans alive only to allow the forest to take us now.

I just hoped the grudge Millicent was holding wouldn't compromise those protections. My stinging finger made me imagine her opening the window in the middle of the night and sliding my bed toward it.

Feeling stupid, I whispered an apology to the wallpaper just to be safe. Then I pulled the heavy burgundy drapes across the glass.

The lamps on the wall brightened to compensate.

Ameline and I stared at each other in shared disquiet.

Bryn said, "That's convenient," and threw herself onto the bed nearest the window. "This one's mine."

I wasn't going to argue.

Ameline eyed the remaining options. "Do you mind if I take the bed closest to the door?"

That left me with the bed in the middle, but I was used to sharing my sleeping space. "Sure."

I walked over and absently poked the mattress. None of us had brought any more than we could strap to our bodies. It had seemed wasteful to take supplies from our families—especially when those supplies had been provided by the beings behind the runegate in the first place.

The same went for taking any precious resources we'd scavenged from the city. What was the point when for all we'd known we'd be dead by sundown?

Then again, from what Bryn had said of her family situation, maybe she just hadn't wanted to bring anything else.

Now that it appeared we would live at least a little longer, I wished I'd brought some of my favorite books with me.

Bryn had stayed on her own mattress for less than thirty seconds and was now squatting by the fireplace, coaxing a flame to life.

I pushed my regret aside. "Want a hand?"

"No. I love fires."

The way she said it made me nervous, but the room was chilly, so I opted for gratitude. With nothing else to do, I knelt to open the trunk at the foot of my bed.

The lid was made of polished timber with an intricately carved hunting scene depicted across its surface. Two men on horseback with cruel-looking spears faced down a snarling, winged lion. The image was arresting in a violent sort of way.

The heavy lid required some heft to flip upward. I'd expected to see the bottom, but the trunk was full. Rich black and deep blue fabric, soft and silky to the touch, occupied most of the space. Handling it gently, I lifted out the top garment, wondering whom it belonged to. Had the last person to use this room left it behind? I couldn't imagine them doing so willingly. The feel and weave of the fabric was far finer than any I'd ever seen.

Ameline's soft exclamation drew my attention. She was holding an identical bundle of midnight-blue cloth. And when we shook them out, they revealed themselves to be fitted shirts with FIRSTBORN ACADEMY stitched across the breast in golden thread.

Uniforms? Glennys *had* insinuated we were students before, but could this place really be some sort of educational institution? And if so, what the heck were we here to learn?

I went through the rest of the trunk, trying to glean what I could from the clothes inside. There were three shirts, three pairs of fitted black pants, one belt, underclothes, a set of sturdy boots, and a heavy, hooded cloak.

The cloak was a relief since the other clothes seemed far too thin to ward off the late-autumn cold.

I was less excited to find the crimson ties at the bottom of the chest. Seriously? We'd surrendered our lives to these unknown beings, and they wanted us to wear *ties*?

Oddly enough, the garments seemed sized to our different body shapes. Bryn's were short, mine long, and Ameline's a touch looser to fit her curves. Even the boots looked to be a good fit. As if they knew we were coming. As if they knew which beds we would each choose.

I shrugged off the tension gathering between my shoulder blades. It was probably a coincidence.

Then again, the wallpaper could feel, the building could bite, and I was in way over my head.

# CHAPTER 5

A growl made me start—an indication of just how creeped out I was feeling because the noise was only Ameline's stomach.

"You guys ready to look for the dining hall?" I asked. "Maybe we can find someone there who knows what the hell's going on."

Humans had been sending firstborns through the runegates for thirty-seven years. Hundreds or maybe thousands of kids. If we *weren't* here to die, surely one of the prior year's students could give us the lowdown on our new lives.

"That'd be nice," Bryn commented. "It can't be good that the golin avoided telling us *anything* about our new overlords."

I wished she'd stop calling them that.

"Why be so evasive if they aren't dreadful?"

The same question had been playing on my mind.

Along with about a million others. But I didn't want Ameline to stress any more than she already was, so I just said, "Let's go and find out."

As promised, the manor *didn't* bite us on our way out. The door had stayed conveniently visible and opened just fine when we turned the handle.

Which left the problem of where to go.

The hallway continued in two directions, and we'd passed several intersecting corridors as we'd followed Glenn and Glennys. There were no handy arrows like the ones I'd seen still clinging to the walls of old office buildings either.

I peered closer at part of the wallpaper that had just moved. It was a strange half-goat, half-man creature, and he was making a very rude gesture.

I swung about in shock, wanting someone to confirm I wasn't hallucinating. "Hey, this little faun thing is flipping me off!"

Ameline hustled over and squinted. "No, he isn't. He's just pointing right. Maybe he's giving us directions."

I looked again. Sure enough, he was pointing right. But he bared his teeth at me when I leaned close.

Shaking my head, I agreed to go the way he indicated. But only because he'd offered the direction to Ameline. I had a sneaking suspicion that if I'd been by myself, I ought to choose the *opposite* way any wallpaper figures directed me.

Millicent must not have accepted my apology.

We fell into a rhythm, Ameline leading the way and peering at the wallpaper anytime we came to an intersection. I pointedly *avoided* looking. And we were led to a grand and cavernous room filled with delicious aromas and... not much else.

While there were chairs and tables enough for two hundred, only a handful of teenagers huddled around two separate tables. Close enough for comfort. Distant enough to signal the two groups wanted nothing to do with each other.

Along the far wall was a serve-yourself selection of food and crockery. Ethereal music played quietly in the background, and no one was around to supervise, human or otherwise.

The walls were covered in wallpaper, of course.

Ameline's stomach growled again, so we went to the food first. The individual dishes were covered by mesh domes woven of delicate silver strands. And either the food had just been cooked, or those domes did something to keep it fresh. Because every option looked and smelled amazing.

If only I was more hungry. The strain of the day had sapped my appetite. We served ourselves— Ameline and I dishing only small portions, Bryn heaping her plate high—and made our way to the nearest table.

"Is this seat free?" Ameline asked.

Back home, whenever we'd needed a favor, we made sure she did the asking. With her angelic face and halo of golden hair, she always got better results than I did. Even before she'd grown generous curves.

The self-designated leader of the group—a boy with a square jaw and blue eyes that matched Ameline's in hue but not in warmth—sized us up.

"For *you* it's available," he said with a wide smile at my friend. "My name's Jayden, by the way." Then he focused on Bryn and me. "You two can move along."

We *all* moved along. I made sure to kick the leg of Jayden's chair as I passed.

"Whoops, so clumsy of me."

The purple fruit juice he'd been about to drink made a satisfying mess over his white T-shirt, and his curses followed me over to the other table.

I grinned.

The second group made room for us. Three guys and two girls, who were fresh arrivals like we were. They'd come from three other survivor cities dotted across America, and since stepping through the runegates, they'd had a similar experience as our own.

Except for the stabbing-the-walls part.

I was beginning to feel embarrassed about that.

A new guy entered the dining hall and made straight for the food without pausing to get his bearings. He was attractive in a hardened sort of way, with a lean, muscular build, hair clipped short, and the kind of face structure that spoke of strength and stubbornness.

But what interested me most was the way he carried himself, the way he moved. There was a surety to his actions the rest of us lacked. Like maybe he knew what was going on.

Or he was superb at bluffing.

"There's room at our table," I offered as he turned from the serving station.

But he shook his head and proceeded to wolf down his food still standing. He finished the meal in so short a time it didn't seem possible, set down the plate, and strode out of the room.

Purpose. That was what his movements had that ours lacked. He'd moved with purpose rather than uncertainty.

I wanted to know why. But unless I was going to chase him down the corridor and tackle him to the floor, that would have to wait. Tempting, but no. First impressions might matter.

I turned my attention back to our tablemates.

No, they hadn't come across anyone who'd arrived last year. Or the years before that.

No, they hadn't been told any more than we had by Glenn and Glennys. Three of the five had barely been brave enough to speak to the "monster" at all.

And yes, they thought this whole setup seemed off.

Tension made their movements twitchy, their appetites small, and their desire to talk shrivel.

If only Jayden at the other table had been affected the same way.

"My dad's the mayor of Lewiston," he was telling the others. "And he's going to send in a whole team of his best men with all the gear they've salvaged to get me back."

"But you know what happens if someone breaks the Agreement," one of his companions protested. "Even if they can locate you and then make it through who-knows-how-many miles of forest, your whole bloodline will die."

Jayden sneered, revealing something green stuck in his teeth. "You reckon we haven't thought of that, Wyatt? My dad has read the Agreement word for word, and it only stipulates seventeen-year-olds go *through* the runegate. Not that they can never return. So we'll be honoring the letter of the Agreement, and whatever beasts think they have us over a barrel won't have a leg to stand on."

He shoved another forkful into his mouth and chewed for a while before adding, "The magic enforcing the Agreement isn't smart. That's why you have to send a firstborn through in their seventeenth year even if they died as an infant." He chewed a bit more. "So stick with me, and I might let you lot come along."

I didn't know it yet, but Jayden would be the first to die.

Right then, I just thought he was an idiot. If it were that simple, someone in the thirty-seven years we'd been sending them would've returned by now. News didn't travel fast anymore, but a story like that would spread.

Even so, I tucked the idea of a possible loophole into the back of my mind. I'd promised my own father I'd return if I possibly could. Maybe I'd have a chance to use it someday.

Gradually the other kids left the dining hall until Ameline, Bryn, and I were the only ones left.

I pushed away my plate.

"What do you think is really going on here? Are we at some kind of weird alien boarding school where attendance is mandatory and failure to show up means death for you and your family?"

I shook my head. "It makes no sense. And if this *is* some sort of academy, where the hell are last year's students?"

Ameline nudged food around her own half-finished plate. "Nothing makes sense about this place."

Bryn had been packing away her meal with zero sign of the suppressed appetite affecting the rest of us. "Tell me about it," she said. "But at least it's interesting."

She speared a roasted root vegetable that had been drizzled with honey and salt. "And the food is wonderful. If you ask me, we should enjoy it for however long it lasts."

I supposed I *had* asked her, and there was wisdom in her approach. But I'd come here with three purposes, and none of them were to enjoy myself.

First, I would pay the blood price for my family to live out their lives in relative peace and protection. If Jayden was to be believed, that part was done as soon I'd stepped through the runegate.

Second, I was here to protect Ameline. We'd vowed

we would face whatever would come together. But she was good and kind and gentle, and I wanted with every part of my being to preserve that.

I wasn't like Ameline. I wasn't nearly as nice. I'd been born hard somehow. Perhaps more like my mother than my softhearted father. And I felt deep down in my soul that it was so I could protect the precious yet vulnerable people in this world.

Which led me to my third purpose for being here. The one I'd spent my life preparing for. The one I'd never admitted to anyone.

I was going to learn about the bastards who demanded the firstborn price. And I was going to take them down.

# CHAPTER 6

The question at the forefront of my mind was whether we'd survive long enough to achieve *anything* besides my first goal.

Were the previous years' firstborns already dead?

Was Fletcher—the boy next door who'd been as warm and wonderful as Ameline—lying motionless in some unmarked grave?

My heart twisted.

But I was trying not to jump to conclusions. I'd never expected to learn everything I needed to know my first day here. *Patience*, I chided myself.

We left the dining hall and spotted the golin leading a trio of girls down the corridor. On impulse, I jogged to catch up.

Glenn eyeballed me. "Is your room not to your liking then? Not enough holes in the walls perhaps?"

Glennys sighed. "What can we help you with, child?"

I ignored Glenn and tried to channel Ameline's charming sweetness—the stuff that made everyone warm to her.

"Well, madam, sir, I mean, um—"

"Glennys."

"Right. Glennys. Well, we were just wondering, where are the other kids? The ones that were sent last year? Or the year before that?"

The two heads shared a glance.

"You humans are so impatient," muttered Glenn.

Glennys smiled in a way that was probably supposed to be comforting.

"Glenn's right. For a *rare* change. You'll have your questions answered in good time when the masters will it. Until then, don't you worry about the others. Get some sleep."

Glenn's lips pulled back in a smile too, but I didn't think his was intended to be comforting.

"You'll need it."

Well, that was about as useful as a car without fuel. Temporarily defeated, I jogged back to my roommates and filled them in on the conversation.

Ameline then made herself invaluable by asking the wallpaper's directions to the girls' bathroom.

A stack of towels and toiletries greeted us as we stepped through the door—which hadn't even required blood to enter. We helped ourselves, relieved we hadn't made a grievous mistake in leaving the supplies with our families.

I was also relieved to find normal-looking toilets and delighted to find they flushed. People back home had repurposed some of LA's old water towers to give us a form of electricity-less running water. But only a few of the wealthiest family homes had access. The rest of us had to manually fill our toilet cisterns with buckets lugged from the nearest rainwater-collection tank.

Far more magical than the toiletries and flushing toilets, however, was the line of shower stalls. Ameline tried one of the taps, and water poured from the shower-head above.

She ran her fingers through the stream and gasped. "You're not going to believe this. It's *hot.*"

My jaw dropped. I'd grown up washing with a pot of water heated over the fire. It took forever to warm, and we had to repeat the process five times so every family member could take a turn.

I rushed into a second shower stall and stripped off my clothes. It sounded like Bryn was doing the same.

Ameline moaned in bliss, already under hers. "Oh my goodness, it's *amazing.*"

I turned on the tap and danced impatiently for it to warm up.

It didn't.

I tried the other tap.

Still cold.

In the stall next to me, Bryn said, "Mine's not working."

That's when I put two and two together.

"Dammit, Millicent. I'm sorry about the wall, okay? I didn't know!"

The water, if anything, grew colder.

Teeth chattering, I rinsed myself off as quick as I could, muttering about grudge-holding buildings.

Ameline came out of her stall with rosy cheeks and a smile she tried to hide. But she kindly offered her finger to the serpent so we could enter our dorm room without further bloodshed.

The sky had grown dark behind the drapes, but Bryn's fire was blazing merrily, filling the space with toasty warmth. It was particularly welcome after my freezing shower.

I covered a yawn. I'd barely been able to sleep last night and had woken before dawn to squeeze the most out of my final hours with my family.

I wasn't the only one yawning either. So after trying and failing to find a way of adjusting the lighting, the three of us crawled into bed.

The lamps dimmed and went out.

All right then.

I wondered again how so many firstborns could disappear from this manor without a trace. Where were they now? What had happened to them?

And what did it mean that everyone we'd spoken to had come from cities around North America? Were there other academies like this one? Was the Firstborn Agreement limited to this continent? Or most horrifying of all—were there no surviving human settlements anywhere else on earth?

Realizing I'd never get any sleep with thoughts like that, I took a leaf out of Bryn's book and focused on the positive.

The mattress was incredibly soft, the blankets warm, and the wallpaper a little less creepy in the dark.

Or was that *more* creepy in the dark?

I needed to stop thinking about the wallpaper.

But when I managed to quash that train of thought, I found myself yearning for my lumpy old mattress at home.

Mila would have crawled in beside me by now, her small and squirmy body warming me inside and out. She had her own mattress but preferred to share mine most nights.

The room was cozy thanks to Bryn's fire, and there was nothing wrong with my body temperature. But the hollow ache in my chest persisted until exhaustion at last overcame me.

# CHAPTER 7

Humans say magic broke the world.

According to my grandmother, the invaders claim that magic merely re-formed it.

Either way, when the world walkers and their entourage of monsters came, humankind drew closer to extinction than any other time since Adam ate that damned apple.

The monsters and magic killed millions. Our desperate acts with nuclear weapons killed more. And the shuddering ripples of life without the technology we'd learned to depend on—the subsequent disease outbreaks and food shortages and chaos—slaughtered most of all.

At first humankind fought back.

The survivors surrendered.

Before communication failed, they'd seen the monstrous devouring darkness in Europe wipe out all life on the continent. Seen the walkers clearing still more territory for themselves, driving out the humans and animals that had once called it home and burning their settlements to the ground.

In the territory that remained, the earth itself had become hostile to us, morphing with the invaders' magic into something hungry and alien, and swarming with monsters that were even more so.

The richest and most powerful humans left on spaceships to settle on Mars or hastily built space stations. Grandmother said there were rumors at the time that they were working on a solution to save the rest of us.

They did not come back.

So the remnants of humankind clustered in the concrete jungles made by their ancestors and slowly starved or were plucked away one by one by the monsters roaming the forests.

Until the *others* offered the Firstborn Agreement. They would provide food, provisions, and protection within our concrete walls on one condition. That every firstborn child, regardless of gender, mental faculties, or physical health, would be sent to the *others* in their seventeenth year.

On pain of death.

Under the circumstances, it seemed a worthy trade. One does not have to look far into human history to learn that incessant, gnawing hunger and the fear of dying drive people to do unspeakable things.

That was three generations ago now. I hadn't been born yet. But my grandmother told me the tales until she passed, and then my father took over the mantle of storyteller. Historian. Teacher. My mother said nothing at all, pressing her lips together the way she always did when she was displeased about something.

Understanding the history of the sacrifice I was destined to make had helped me accept it.

I'd known it was coming, and known *why* it was coming, for each of my seventeen years. And I'd found a peace in that. A purpose even.

But when I was literally flipped out of my bed the first morning after stepping through the runegate, that acceptance was sorely tested.

My soft, comfortable mattress had abruptly decided to stand upright.

I groaned and rubbed the parts of me that had been the first to hit the floor. On my right, Bryn was suffering through a similar wake-up call. On my left, Ameline's mattress rocked her gently awake.

Guess that meant Millicent hadn't given up her grudge overnight then.

Noises through the door suggested we weren't the only ones who'd been woken. We'd slept in our soft new uniforms for want of clean sleepwear, and they were miraculously unwrinkled now. So all we needed to do was pull on boots and belts and run hasty fingers through our hair before we were presentable enough to learn what was happening.

Or so I thought.

Until one of the ties I'd left in the bottom of my trunk caught me around the neck as I reached for the door handle.

A wise person knows when to pick their battles. Ameline and I straightened each other's ties, Bryn insisted hers preferred to be askew, and we finally burst into the hallway.

Other kids, all of them likewise wearing uniforms, were walking in a single direction down the corridor. There were far more people than we'd seen yesterday, and I wondered if we'd found the missing firstborns from previous years. Excitement fluttered in my chest.

Maybe we were about to get answers.

I needed to use the bathroom, but curiosity urged me forward. The three of us followed the crowd.

We made our way downstairs, passed the turnoff that led to the dining hall, and turned instead into a wider, grander passage with vaulted ceilings and nook after nook of antique treasures.

Over the sea of heads, I could see a set of imposing double doors and Glenn and Glennys beside it. The golin said something to the nearest students, then threw the doors open.

Beyond them was the manicured lawn I'd glimpsed from our bedroom window.

Outside.

A mere two hundred yards from the perilous forest.

To my amazement, the first students stepped

through the doorway, and the crowd resumed its forward momentum. Kids hesitated but were urged on by Glenn or Glennys. I guessed it was a combination of muttered threats and kind assurances that drove them onward. But no screams of terror came from those milling on the lawn, and slowly the pace sped up.

I was beginning to regret my shortsightedness in not having gone to the bathroom.

When our trio reached the doors, the fresh morning air swept over me.

"What's happening?" I asked Glennys.

"Your first class. Hurry now. Professor Cricklewood doesn't like tardiness."

Bryn leaned past me. "Did we miss breakfast?"

"Don't worry about that, child. You'll want an empty stomach for this lesson."

With those foreboding words, we walked down the manor's steps and onto the grass.

Everything I'd spied from our dorm room seemed bigger out here. The gardens, the topiary cats, the lake, and most especially the imposing wall of the forest hemming us in.

A wizened old man with a long white beard and an ornate walking staff half again his height approached the group, heedless of the swirling mists drifting in from the woods.

His watery blue eyes and kindly human features made him feel comfortable and familiar in this strange place. And I took a half step toward him, wondering if he might be the one to finally make sense of what was happening to us.

Then he opened his mouth.

"Look sharp, you liver-licking, shrimp-for-brains maggots! When I tell you to run, your hooves better be flying or I'll teach you to regret it, you hear?"

He paced back and forth in front of our gobsmacked group, wielding his staff like a weapon.

Which upon closer inspection, it was. The spiked top was not decorative.

"I will force you sloppy snot-burgers into shape if I have to shove you through the meat grinder myself. Notice I said *you* and not me because I could lap you lazy scum-suckers running backward with my eyes closed!"

A poor hapless girl raised her hand. "Sir, I was just wondering, sir, um, whether we could run inside where it's safe?"

He thumped his staff viciously into the ground at her feet, and she scrambled backward until she hit the kid behind her.

"You want to stay safe?" the professor roared. "Then. Follow. My. Orders!"

He paused for a moment, then conceded, "And stay on this side of the sentinel hedge cats."

His voice reverted to a drill-sergeant shout. "Now run or *I'll* eat you."

A few of the students chuckled, but I had the distinct impression Cricklewood wasn't joking.

I ran.

The grass felt strange under my feet. Soft and kind of springy compared to the asphalt and concrete I usually ran on.

Back home, I hadn't known what to prepare for, so I'd tried to be prepared for anything.

Every day I jogged up the stairwell of the tallest remaining skyscraper, then ran a seven-mile route around the safe areas of the city. If someone in the community had a feasibly useful skill, I offered to perform odd jobs for them in exchange for learning it. I also read everything I could get my hands on.

The running, hard labor, and skill acquisition was harder than the reading. It was no burden to lose myself in stories of the Before. But I made sure I did both. And that discipline put me in good stead now.

I was at the head of the group as we jogged around the manicured lawn. After half a dozen laps, the only person beside me was the guy who'd caught my attention in the dining hall. The one who'd moved differently from everyone else. Mr. Knows-Something-We-Don't.

We ran another dozen laps, the other kids falling farther behind.

I checked on my running companion. Out here in the daylight, his eyes were more gold than brown, and there was life on his face that had been lacking last night.

Like me, he was barely breathing hard, his strong

athletic build demolishing the miles with ease. Plenty of capacity to talk then.

The real question was whether he'd cooperate. Time to find out.

"I'm Nova," I said.

He didn't respond.

I made my voice honey-sweet. "You don't have to answer if you're too short of breath."

He shot me a look.

"I'm Klay."

Well, that was two more words than I'd gotten out of him in the dining hall. He had an unusual accent too. One I couldn't place.

"How long have you been here, Klay?"

"Since yesterday."

Damn. Not that I'd really expected him to say otherwise, but if *he* wasn't a firstborn from a prior year's intake, then none of the kids puffing behind us were.

Then again, I wasn't sure I believed he'd only just arrived.

"Do you know something the rest of us don't?"

I glanced over to gauge his reaction.

"The balance of probabilities would suggest yes," he informed me, and maybe his lips curved a fraction as he said it. "You'll have to be more specific."

I bit back a growl, wishing Ameline was here to win him over. Rapport building was *not* in my wheelhouse.

*All right, smartass.* "Do you know what's going on here? Who the beings behind the Agreement are? And why they'd want to steal human firstborns from their families just to make them run around in circles for no apparent reason?"

"I know you should focus on Professor Cricklewood's lessons if you want to live," Klay said.

Then he put on a burst of speed in an unsubtle signal our conversation was over.

I could've caught up. But it wouldn't have made him any more accommodating, and I wasn't sure how long this exercise would go on. Smarter to pace myself.

Half a dozen laps later, Cricklewood whistled shrilly. "That's enough of that, you miserable manticore snacks! I want to see thirty-seven push-ups. Seventy-four for anyone who doesn't complete them in a timely manner."

*Thirty-seven?* What was wrong with three dozen?

Was this guy an eccentric professor or—I swallowed as a new possibility occurred to me—a world walker?

Walkers in the stories were always beautiful. Cricklewood wasn't. But he was a long way from your average human too. Maybe like Glenn and Glennys he'd been gifted by the "masters" here with powers.

Like the ability to curse a mean streak. And terrify teenagers into exercising first thing in the morning.

We dropped where we were, scattered around the track, and did as we'd been ordered. Most kids were strong enough from hand-hauling water and supplies around our communities. Life was tougher after the invasion. But as the son of a mayor, Jayden must have lived a life of privilege. His face was red and his arms were wobbling before he was halfway done. I knew this because I'd been about to lap him, and that meant he was disappointingly nearby.

Cricklewood stalked over to Jayden and rammed his staff into the earth an inch from the boy's straining fingers. "Congratulations. Just for making me pity you, I'll allow *you* to do seventy-four."

Jayden's cheeks darkened further, and he sat up. "Get lost. I haven't even had breakfast yet."

Cricklewood's voice turned real quiet.

"Keep. Going."

But Jayden crossed his arms. "No. You can yell all you want, old man, but you can't make me."

The elderly professor smiled then. "Oh but I can."

And I watched as Jayden's body jerkily returned to doing push-ups.

After runegates and sentient buildings and surviving the night this close to the forest without being eaten, it was hardly the largest display of magic I'd witnessed. But it sent unease spreading through my stomach all the same. Perhaps because it was the first time I'd seen magic used *against* us.

Well, apart from Millicent flinging me out of bed and sabotaging my shower.

Jayden's eyes were wide, almost bulging, and his lips appeared to be glued shut. But that didn't stop him whimpering when his underdeveloped muscles began to cramp.

I looked away. I didn't like Jayden, but I didn't want to watch Cricklewood bully him either.

Bryn was one of the other forerunners and completed her push-ups at the same time I did. Ameline had settled somewhere in the middle of the group. She might be curvy, but she wasn't as soft as she looked.

"All right!" Cricklewood's shout interrupted my survey. "Now that you've warmed up, we'd usually move on to weapons training. But as you pitiful wet-noodle-armed wretches have so aptly demonstrated, you don't have a hope in hell of waving a sword without skewering yourselves. So you get to repeat all that again instead. Now run!"

Some kids whimpered, others groaned, but we all got up and started running. Even Jayden.

I was happy to move my legs again. It gave my mind time to churn over the implications. *Weapons training? Sword?* Were our new "masters" trying to make an army out of us?

The idea was so preposterous I almost snorted. It was more likely they were torturing us for sport. And yet… if there was any truth in the idea, it wasn't funny at all.

We ran and did strength exercises and then ran again.

By the time Cricklewood called for a stop, almost everyone had made at least one trip to vomit into the bushes. The ones near the manor rather than the forest, naturally.

Ameline was pale and shaky. Bryn was sweat-soaked

but determined. Jayden looked like he might have been crying. And knows-something-we-don't Klay was barely winded.

Jerk.

Or maybe that was just my competitive side talking because I wanted to be the best.

I had to excel. How else could I convince myself I had some hope of pulling off my wild scheme?

And how else could I convince the targets of my scheme that I was willing and worthy and they should trust me with the intel that might bring them down?

Of course at this stage, we still hadn't caught so much as a glimpse of those unknown targets.

Cricklewood eyeballed the ragged assembly of exhausted firstborns.

"I suppose congratulations are in order"—a few heads lifted in hope—"for being the most pathetic group of wretches I've ever had the displeasure of laying eyes on. Now get out of my sight. Breakfast is waiting for those that can stomach it. Meanwhile, I'll try to forget your appalling performance so you can impress me anew this evening."

There was a collective groan among my peers.

Few of us could've predicted the day was only going to get worse.

# CHAPTER 8

Cricklewood had made it clear that showering would have to wait, which meant we were a sweaty and sorry lot of humans who trudged into the dining hall.

But whatever our uniforms were made of, they must have had magical properties because the enclosed space did not smell of body odor, dirt, or vomit. Instead, the delicious scents of breakfast wafted over us.

I'd darted away to use the bathroom and was now in a state to find the food appealing.

Glenn and Glennys were serving—helping the line move faster than it otherwise might with so many of us barely able to lift our arms—and repeating instructions to each student who came by.

"You have fifteen minutes before your next lesson. So eat quickly, and the wallpaper will direct you to your respective classrooms."

Since Ameline, Bryn, and I didn't know if we'd be in

the same class, we separated as soon as we'd devoured our fresh-baked seed bread and platter of fruit. Which left me to face the wallpaper alone.

A unicorn tossed its head and pointed with its obsidian horn. A vaguely humanoid lump of a creature that looked like it had been molded by a half-blind artist pointed with his poorly formed finger. A hippogriff ruffled its feathers and refused to offer direction at all. And something that looked like the offspring of a confused giraffe and ostrich pointed with its feathered hoof.

At least one of them was lying.

Because I wound up at the dead end of a quiet corridor, and by the time I'd retraced my steps and found the right room, I was late for class.

Thank you, Millicent.

Not the first impression I wanted to make. I could only hope this professor would be more sympathetic than Cricklewood.

In case they weren't, I drew in a deep, bracing breath, then pushed open the door. At least it didn't require blood for entrance.

As soon as I slipped inside, I forgot about the professor's personality.

An invisible line divided the classroom down the middle. The humans were on one side, including Bryn, who must have been late too because she was only just sitting down, as well as Jayden, Klay, and a girl who'd thrown up three times this morning.

On the other side of the classroom, though the seated figures were human in appearance and wearing the same uniforms as the rest of us, something *other* made the hair on my arms stand up.

Instincts buried so deep that I barely understood them. But on some primal level, I did understand.

They were predators, and I was prey.

World walkers.

I'd never seen one in my life, yet I knew it with utter certainty.

I glanced toward the professor and saw he was a walker too.

Which meant... our Agreement was with the walkers. The most monstrous of all the monsters that had brought about the end of the world as we knew it.

Except perhaps for the devouring darkness that destroyed Europe.

Oh, they didn't *look* like monsters. My gaze drank them in. The male with ebony curls and eyes like wildfire. The female with hair the color of frost and flawless skin nearly as pale. The male at the back with cheekbones sharp enough to cut and eyes so blue they put the sky to shame.

I hated them.

Despite their looks, they weren't angels or gods. They were beautiful, bloodthirsty monsters.

Somehow the fact they resembled us made it worse.

I knew that wasn't logical. Knew too that there were plenty of monsters in history who were one hundred percent human. Yet fear and loathing and a sense of inevitability tightened my gut.

In that moment, it felt like I'd always believed somewhere in my core that the Agreement must be with the walkers.

But why?

What did they want with us? Why had they offered the Agreement when they did? Why had they offered it at all? Why hadn't they offered it sooner? Before most of the human, bird, and animal populations had been wiped out?

I'd stood frozen for too long. Students on both sides of the classroom were murmuring. And the professor was frowning in my direction.

"You're late, Nova."

How did he know my name?

"Kindly find a seat and don't delay us more than you already have."

I swallowed. The walkers noticed the involuntary movement, I was sure of it.

They were predators, and I was prey.

But I was not helpless prey.

I stiffened my spine and found a seat right in the center of that invisible divide. Let them stare at me. Let them whisper. Let them wonder. I could handle it.

I'd been preparing my whole life for this. Training from the moment my mind had evolved enough to grasp the core concepts. To make that secret vow to myself.

I let my hair fall across my cheek to hide the determination setting my jaw and the tug of satisfaction on my lips.

Let them wonder. But let them not wonder why the hunted, helpless human had other things on her mind than running.

There was a fountain pen and notebook on the desk in front of me. I picked them up and copied down the title of today's lesson in indigo ink.

The Strategies of Guerrilla Warfare.

The teacher rose to his feet with liquid grace. He was tall and striking with skin the color of burnt umber and a penetrating gaze that swept over the assembled teenagers.

"I am Professor Dunraven. And the next time a student is late to my class, they will be punished."

Mercifully, he did not direct that comment solely to me.

"Now, I'm aware this is your first classroom lecture, so I will explain a few things about this institution before we delve into today's topic."

The walkers, I noticed, sat unnaturally still.

I tried to ignore them.

Dunraven went on. "You are about to commence an intense, three-month training and trial period, at the end of which, only the best will continue with the academy."

"What happens to the others?" Jayden interrupted.

Dunraven's dark amber eyes rested on him a moment too long. "You will find out if you fail."

The knot in my stomach wound tighter. And I vowed then that I would be one of the best. One of the kids they selected. And I'd make damn sure Ameline was one of them too. Somehow.

But what Dunraven said next was worse.

"Not everyone is expected to survive the training. We do our best to keep casualties to a minimum, but we care more about the results than individuals."

His gaze swept around the classroom again, meeting our shocked stares without flinching. As if he hadn't just delivered a potential death sentence for the sake of *results*.

"So I suggest you apply yourselves."

Again, I felt a strange sense of inevitability. I'd never expected my life after stepping through the runegate to be anything but harsh. That was one of the reasons I'd worked so hard to prepare for it.

Now I would learn whether that preparation had been enough. It would *have* to be enough.

"Both walkers and humans are expected to work together. The staff knows there is bad blood between the species, but we don't want to hear about it. Here at this academy, you are on the same side—or you will fail. Do I make myself clear?"

A few heads nodded woodenly, and that was enough to satisfy Dunraven. He clasped his hands.

"Good. Then allow me tell you about the Clarion war and the strategies we can derive from it."

A walker raised his hand and waited until Dunraven nodded in his direction.

"Seriously, sir? We learned this when we were toddlers still growing in our teeth—"

Dunraven spoke with a quiet calm far more intimidating than Cricklewood's shouts.

"Then consider this a lesson in patience."

And everyone, walker and human alike, kept their complaints to themselves after that.

# CHAPTER 9

We were given no time to absorb the revelations regarding the walkers or the academy.

The knowledge that we were here to be trained and tested.

That we were supposed to ally with the beings that had destroyed our world.

And that some of us wouldn't make it.

Professor Dunraven flooded us with historic battles on other worlds, illustrating tactics a smaller force could use against a much larger one. It was a topic I'd barely scratched the surface of in my own reading, and it was all I could do to take notes so I could study them later. Then a mournful chiming of bells announced the end of the lesson.

Dunraven halted midsentence and dismissed the class.

Well, almost.

"Bryn, Nova, stay behind for a moment please."

We stayed seated as our peers shuffled out. I had the urge to clutch my notebook to my chest in some kind of futile defense, but I left it on the desk.

"I heard you upset Millicent," he said, coming over and touching a finger to a blank page of my notebook.

"Yes, sir."

From his finger, green lines spilled onto the paper and arranged themselves until they formed...

A floor plan. Of Millicent Manor, I realized.

He took three steps and did the same for Bryn.

"So you won't be late again," he said.

There was no discernible benevolence in the gesture. He just wanted us to be on time for his class. Yet I felt a surge of gratitude, and it sat uncomfortably indeed to be indebted to a walker.

We thanked him and hurried out in an effort not to be late to our *next* class. The other students had already disappeared.

We paused to stare at our maps.

Dunraven's green lines showed the complex warren of Millicent's two main levels, as well as a set of stairs indicating a basement and the grand set of doors that led outside.

Most of the rooms were unlabeled, but the dormitories, bathrooms, and dining hall were identified in neat green print. There were also five classrooms pinpointed.

Rudimentary Magic; The Strategies of Warfare;

Dangerous Magical Creatures 101; An Introduction to Botany; and Survival Skills.

I knew where we were thanks to the Strategies of Warfare label, but what was my next lesson?

As if in response to my unvoiced question, one of the classrooms shaded green. Okay then.

"What do you have next?" I asked Bryn.

"Survival Skills. You?"

"Dangerous Magical Creatures 101."

Without having to rely on Millicent, we caught up with the other students traveling between classrooms.

The walkers glided through the halls, seemingly unhurried and yet outpacing the scrambling humans who had to check the wallpaper at frequent intervals. Or, in Bryn's and my case, our maps.

I was pleased to make it to my next lesson when half the seats were still empty and even more pleased to learn Ameline was taking the same class. Her face brightened when she saw me.

I sat next to her, choosing the side toward the center of the classroom to show the walkers I was unafraid. "Did you get the same introduction to the academy as we did?"

Her mouth turned down. "I'm guessing so."

I'd worried about that. "How are you holding up?"

She doodled something on her notebook. "My botany teacher was nicer than Cricklewood at least."

I smirked. "That's not saying much."

Her mouth turned upward this time. "I didn't get compared to snail gizzards once."

I laughed and patted her arm, secretly relieved to see her smile. "A definite improvement."

Then our teacher walked into the room. "I am Professor Wilverness, and I will be teaching you the perils and peculiarities of many dangerous magical creatures."

She appeared to be a centaur, or something like it. Her human half had smoky gray skin with a texture reminiscent of bark, an ethereal face, and the most majestic set of antlers I'd ever seen. Her hair, both on her human head and horse's tail, was thick and long, composed of tendrils of green ivy and strings of wildflowers. The horse's coat was green too and had a mossy appearance.

"Who knows what I am?" she asked.

Her voice was dry and whispery, reminding me of wind through leaves. And in her presence, the classroom began to smell like the earth after it rained.

One of the walkers answered. "An Antellian," he said.

"That's right. Antellians are shifters who are able to take any form they like, though in every form they will bear the telltale antlers."

Her hooves clopped quietly against the floorboards as she weaved her way through the desks, allowing us to gawk as she passed.

"Antellians can be extremely dangerous if hungry or

provoked, but they are quite reclusive by nature. So if you do not threaten them or the forest they call their home, it is unlikely you will come to harm. Does anyone know what makes them vulnerable?"

Another walker raised her hand. "The only magic they possess is that of shifting. So while they're fast healers and dangerous foes, a mortal wound will kill them."

"Correct." Wilverness nodded, sending her long hair swaying around her torso. Her tranquil expression gave no sign she was bothered by this academic discussion of murdering her people.

"If you did not already know the answer to that question, you should be taking notes."

I shook myself from my stupor and hurried to write it down. When I looked up, the professor had morphed into a dragon. An *antlered* dragon but a frighteningly realistic one.

Metallic golden scales winked in the sunlight streaming through the arched windows. Wickedly sharp talons dug into the timber floor. And when the creature canted its head to eyeball us, I spied teeth as large as my forearm.

I suddenly understood why this class was held in a room that spanned the full height of the manor. The dragon was so large that when its wings shifted, a breeze stirred my hair.

Wilverness's voice, though, was the same. "I expect everyone will know what this form is."

I sensed rather than saw my peers nod along with me, my eyes fixed on the beast.

"The perils are obvious enough. Dragons possess enormous strength, lethally sharp teeth and talons, the ability to breathe fire, and their scales are almost impervious to harm. They are highly intelligent but rarely ally themselves with other species, and they'll attack almost anything when they're hungry. Would someone care to explain their vulnerabilities?"

I belatedly remembered to sketch and scribble again.

A walker girl with hair as bright as dragon flame answered.

"They're cold-blooded, so if you can cool them down sufficiently, their speed turns sluggish and they can only huff smoke. Then if you can get close with a magical blade, you *might* be able to slay them. Some claim that if you convince them to eat meat laced with dragonbane, that the poison will kill them too."

"That's right, but the dragonbane theory is unsubstantiated. What if your aim is not to kill but to escape or avoid detection?"

I scribbled and sketched furiously as the lesson continued, barely able to keep up with the flood of information. A quick glance while I shook out my cramping hand proved Ameline's sketches were far better than mine. Oh well. Maybe I'd borrow her notes when we tried to memorize this later.

For now, it was all I could do to follow along as Professor Wilverness shifted shapes and explained the dangers, inclinations, potential alliances, vulnerabilities, and best strategies for dealing with each creature. Thank the heavens my pen never seemed to run out of indigo ink.

The professor was like nature itself: beautiful and alluring, but wild and unpredictable too.

Yet she seemed intent on helping us learn, and I wondered why. If the Antellians were reclusive as she claimed, why had she agreed to help the walkers by teaching at this academy? Had they threatened her with something? Stolen her offspring or loved one? Why would she ally herself with the species that wrought so much death and destruction?

"Is anything *not* dangerous?" one of the human kids asked—after a slew of horrifying creatures that made my head spin.

At first I'd been excited by the information. Maybe a human could survive in the forest if they knew the ins and outs of the creatures that dwelled within. However, as the class stretched on, my excitement waned. It was all very well to know the best way to neutralize a chimera was to rub the spot on its belly that released copious amounts of endorphins, but if you were a human, you'd die long before you reached it.

In answer to the kid's question, Wilverness transformed into what looked like a watermelon-sized ball of fluff with tiny hooves.

The class giggled and made *aww* noises before quieting to hear what Wilverness had to say.

"The flum are harmless enough. But they are bitter to eat and not much use for anything except to keep your feet warm during a cold night. Which is why we won't be covering them in this class."

She shifted into a troll. A big brute of a beast with beady yellow eyes and moist gray skin that was not the least bit adorable.

"My job is to prepare you to go out into the world and not become a predator's breakfast. So pay attention, learn which creatures might be persuaded to help you and how to escape the rest, and you *might* survive until lunch."

The human half of the classroom tittered nervously. One of the walkers yawned. But none went so far as to express boredom. Maybe Wilverness had won their respect too.

A human in the front row raised his hand. "What about the devouring monster that destroyed Europe?"

I saw Klay straighten in his seat.

The walkers stiffened.

Tension settled like a blanket over the room.

Of all the things the walkers had unleashed on our world, this, *this* was the most unforgivable.

Professor Wilverness had morphed back into her centaur form and was standing still and upright, like a deer on the verge of running.

"It is known as the Malus," she said softly. "The word translates roughly to *Devourer*."

"What are its vulnerabilities?" the same kid asked.

"None. That I know of." She seemed to gather herself. "But the Malus is not yet on this continent, otherwise you'd already be dead. Therefore, it is beyond the scope of this introductory class."

A shudder rippled along her flank.

"Those of you who continue at the academy may learn about it next term."

And then the mournful bells broke the spell and called us onward to our next lesson.

# CHAPTER 10

As the day wore on, it grew increasingly clear that not everyone felt the way I did toward the walkers.

Some of my female classmates giggled and swished their hair, sneaking covert glances at the beautiful monsters. A few of the guys sent them lovelorn stares or tried to show off by flexing their muscles or their egos.

Had they forgotten what the walkers had done to our world? Or was the unparalleled beauty of these walker teenagers enough to make them brush the past aside?

I'd never understood why people put so much stock in appearance. My grandmother had been blind, and she'd been the best judge of character I knew.

Other classmates wore their hatred for the walkers openly as if it were a badge of honor. Those kids stared too, but it was with clenched fists and faces tight with anger.

But no matter which side individuals aligned with, they still traipsed obediently from class to class.

What else could we do? There was nowhere to run except the lethal forest. The only escape offered there was death. And none of us had missed what Cricklewood had done to Jayden. They could *force* us to obey them if we didn't cooperate.

Besides, as confounding and dangerous as our new lives were, the academy was better than most of the scenarios we'd had seventeen years to dream up.

But it didn't seem to matter that every one of us— no matter how we felt about the academy or the walkers —were stuck in the same boat. Battle lines were being drawn. Cliques were being formed. Our human classmates were dividing themselves between hatred and infatuation.

My roommates and I landed somewhere in the middle. Ameline pointed out over lunch that if the walker students were as young as they looked, they'd had no more involvement in the invasion than we had. Bryn bristled, not over their past actions but the fact they possessed all this incredible magic and yet the best thing they'd found to do with it was "sit around and look tragically bored."

As for me, I hid my own feelings deep inside. But my decision to seat myself in the gap between walkers and humans in the classrooms had been noted by both extremes.

The haters called me a walker lover. The infatuated sized me up like I was the competition.

I ignored both groups.

Part of me was aware that at seventeen, navigating teenage politics and young love should have been my biggest concerns. I'd read plenty of books from the Before demonstrating that. But romance and popularity had never been high on my agenda. I had bigger concerns. And I didn't resent it.

Being raised as a sacrifice—being honored and grieved and cherished and isolated—knowing my path was not my own to choose, had given me a different perspective.

The element I *did* have control over was what I would do on the path foreordained for me. I'd decided what that would be a long time ago. The only thing left now was to figure out the details.

So I ignored my classmates' fluttering eyelashes and drooling stares. The open glares and poisonous whispers.

The walkers, for their part, showed an utter disregard for their human counterparts. We were beneath them. No more worthy of note than a flea on a mountain lion. Or so they believed.

Good.

It was better that I was underestimated. Overlooked. Ignored. For the most part anyway.

I knew that eventually I'd need a way in. Need to somehow win the regard of a walker so they might spill their secrets to me. But I sensed they'd be far more intrigued if I went against their expectations.

If I acted like they were nothing to me. If I walked among them without showing fear or hatred or attraction. And certainly *without* throwing myself at their feet. Which was lucky, because while I might be able to tuck away my anger nice and neat, I couldn't imagine feigning love for one of the monsters.

I used Dunraven's map to navigate to my next class and soon discovered our Rudimentary Magic teacher's attitude mirrored the walker students'.

Professor Grimwort was tall and angular even by walker standards, the overhead lighting casting his cold blue eyes and the deep hollows of his cheeks in shadow. He stood with unnerving stillness as we filed in, managing to look both bored and utterly contemptuous at the same time.

When everyone was seated and waiting attentively, he roused himself to speak.

"Today I will be teaching the foundations of magic use. Hollows, feel free to pursue your own studies so long as you do it quietly. Humans, pay attention. I don't like to repeat myself."

*Hollows?* I wondered.

A kid who was earnest but not particularly perceptive since he'd sat in the front row put his hand up. "But, sir. How are we supposed to learn magic if we have none?"

Grimwort lifted his hooded eyes heavenward.

"Powers spare me the inquiring human mind. It's like a blunt instrument hammering at the doors of enlightenment, not realizing the way is already open."

The kid shrank back in his seat, and no one so much as cleared their throat in the silence that followed Grimwort's statement.

At last he let out a deeply felt sigh and began to teach.

"Magic is in all things, but for some the path to access it is like a thick veil, never removed, while for others it is like an open archway, inviting and unencumbered. For still others, it is like a river, flowing inexorably through them as naturally as breathing."

Grimwort's gaze pierced the student unfortunate enough to question him.

"Humankind"—he spoke the word like it evoked a bad taste in his mouth—"have always had at least some magic, although the vast majority of you have been unable to access it. But since the world walkers chose to reside here, your world has become more magical. Soaking up our abundance of life magic so that the earth, the trees, and even the humans are becoming more magical with each passing year and generation."

His tone turned scathing again. "Obviously, you have yet to learn how to harness it, but the academy is generously gifting each human student a thaumaturgy rod."

*A what now?*

I wasn't foolish enough to ask the question aloud.

His prominent nose wrinkled. "Or—in accordance with your historic fantasy lore—you may think of it as a thaumaturgy *wand* if it makes it easier to wrap your uncomprehending heads around the concept."

Grimwort muttered something under his breath that sounded like "We might as well arm toddlers with tornadoes." But he walked to the back wall of the classroom and touched his hand to the wallpaper.

The wall rippled, a large section of the wallpaper disappeared, and in its place was a velvet-lined, glass-fronted case displaying row after row of ivory-colored rods about the length of my forearm. Empty sections of velvet indicated that some of the rods—or wands—had already been taken.

Professor Grimwort slid the glass open and raised his voice so it carried across the classroom again.

"Thaumaturgy rods are an aid, a crutch, to allow you to do that which you cannot do on your own. And luckily for you, their use requires little power and even less skill."

He stepped aside and regarded us. "So come and collect one, and take care to treat them with respect, for they are whittled from the bones of our people."

I halted halfway out of my seat. They were made from the *bones of walkers?*

I wasn't the only one who'd frozen at that pronouncement, and Grimwort glowered. "Don't make me remind you that I dislike repeating myself."

We scrambled into action, curiosity as much as obedience spurring us forward.

Upon closer inspection, the rods, or wands, or *bones* were carved into smooth cylinders and etched with runes or letters in a language I didn't recognize. I'd planned to grab the nearest and dash back to my seat as fast as possible, but my hand was drawn to a different wand—four down and two across from the one I'd intended. When I released it from the velvet, it was both weightier and warmer than I'd expected. Like a length of steel that had been warmed by the fire rather than any bone I'd touched.

I opted to count that as a blessing since I *really* didn't want to think about some dead walker's shinbone every time I held the darn thing.

Grimwort waited for us to return to our seats before speaking again. Doubtless aware that we'd be too distracted to listen and, heaven forbid, he might have to repeat himself.

"The process of using your thaumaturgy rods is simple. Imagine what you want to happen—magic you can clearly visualize is easier than something abstract. Gather your will to make it so, and direct the rod at the object you wish to affect. You will find candles in your desk that you are to practice lighting. But before anyone tries *anything*"—he placed emphasis on the last as students began rummaging through their desk contents to find the candle—"there are several warnings you must heed."

He held up a long finger.

"One, while the rods allow you to *access* your magic, they do not provide a pool of magic to draw from. That comes from you. And when your power reservoir is depleted, the rod will draw on your own body's life force."

He raised a second finger.

"Two, that means you must pay strict attention to how you're feeling to learn your own limits and that you *must not* cast anything ambitious or dramatic until you have a firm grasp on your own constraints. Let me be clear. The average human has only a small reservoir of magic, so even several minor enchantments or a single moderate one can deplete you.

"Once your magic pool is empty, any spell you cast will take a physical toll. A little of that will not do any harm beyond what a good sleep can fix, and the body is wise and will try to knock you unconscious before allowing you to draw so much as to be dangerous. But if you attempt a powerful enough enchantment, the momentum of the casting will blow through your body's safeguards and *you will die.*"

Shocked murmurs ran around the classroom, and my fellow human students gripped their wands more loosely. Like they might decide to bite.

Grimwort appeared bored. "Why don't you all repeat this after me: I will not try to cast anything ambitious until I've learned my own limits, otherwise I will die."

In a messy chorus, we echoed the words back to him.

A hint of amusement played across his sharp features.

"Good. Now you may practice lighting your candles. Then snuff it out and do it again. Anyone with an ounce of magic can use the thaumaturgy rods, but the better focused your imagination and the stronger your force of will, the less magic you'll waste in the process.

"Each of you will also have an affinity in a certain area of magic. Within that area, casting will be easier and less costly for you. So strive to identify your affinity and become efficient in your magic use. Especially since you have so little to work with in the first place."

He returned to the front of the classroom and folded himself into the chair behind his desk, apparently done with teaching.

"Oh, and remember to aim your rod at the candle. Millicent will not be pleased if you set the furniture or floor on fire."

# CHAPTER 11

By the time we'd completed our classes, it was all I could do to drag myself to the dining hall. Hours earlier, my right hand had started cramping so badly I'd switched to my left. The result being half a notebook of illegible scrawl I still had to study and get a handle on before lessons began all over again the next day.

It felt impossible. But what choice was there? Ameline and I *needed* to pass the trial phase. Compared to that, sleep was optional.

My fingers were cramping around my fork, my neck had a crick in it, and my legs were still tired from that morning's workout. But my head was in the worst shape of all—so overwhelmed by the influx of information that I didn't trust myself to form coherent sentences.

We were eating dinner in the dining hall—dinner that was probably delicious but I was too tired to taste—

when Cricklewood's voice blasted throughout the manor.

"All students to report to the front lawn in five minutes. Bring your wands. The first trial is about to begin."

The faces around me morphed from hazy exhaustion to horror. I wasn't alone in completely forgetting about Cricklewood's promise to see us again that evening.

*This* evening.

But really? Were they kidding? They expected us to take part in a trial *now*?

As much as I wanted to believe it was some sort of joke, I rose with the other students and shuffled out to the lawn.

The walkers, who'd essentially spent the day lounging around through lessons that were as basic to them as breathing, perked up for the first time.

No need to lay bets on how this was going to go down.

Dunraven and Cricklewood were waiting on the grass.

At least Grimwort wasn't there to add to our humiliation.

Dunraven made a short, sweeping gesture, and a gateway opened into the forest. Unlike the permanent fixture of the runegate in Los Angeles, this one had no physical structure. It was visible only because we could see what was on the other side, as if Dunraven's hand gesture had pulled aside the fabric of reality and created a window.

The professor poked his head through it, a strange and unsettling view from where I was standing. Then his head reappeared and he waved us forward.

Ameline, Bryn, and I stepped through together. There was a moment of skin-crawling darkness, and just like that, we were standing in the middle of the forest.

The sentient, lethal forest.

The thick layer of rotting leaves felt wrong beneath my feet—even more so than the grass we'd run on that morning.

Fickle, slippery, untrustworthy...

It was impossible for me to imagine the desert my grandmother insisted used to surround Los Angeles. Not that we were necessarily *in* that region anymore, but since I had no clue where the academy was, I'd figured I might as well pretend my family wasn't far away. Maybe it would help with how much I missed them.

Yeah right.

Movement rustled around us, and unfamiliar noises made my arms break out in goose bumps. After Wilverness's lesson today, I could imagine all too well the nightmares that might be waiting for us.

Dunraven spoke again, raising his voice to carry to every student—and effectively alerting all the nearby monsters to our location.

"The trials are an opportunity for you to use what you've learned at the academy in a real-world environment. Knowledge, after all, is only powerful when it's applied."

Seriously? We'd been here a single day, and—based on the number of kids who'd pulled their wands from the provided belt-clip holders and were waving them around—I was pretty sure we'd learned just enough to get us into trouble.

"Your trial today is simply to traverse the two miles of wild terrain and make it back to the academy alive. No gateway magic allowed, otherwise everything is acceptable. Speed will be rewarded, but points will also be assigned for interspecies aid. So help each other. Work together. And nobody needs to die."

None of the nervous gigglers chuckled this time. They did not doubt that this was real.

The only good thing about the fear was that it sent adrenaline pumping through our systems, making us more alert, more able to push past the fatigue.

Cricklewood, who was standing beside Dunraven like the wizened crone next to a fairy king, grinned in such a way that it showed every one of his teeth. I'd discovered he was a walker too, just a very old one.

"The pathetic excuse for snail slime who drags them-selves back to the manor grounds *last* will be rewarded with a swim around the frigid lake bright and early tomorrow. So go ahead and surprise me by *not* failing miserably, why don't you?"

Dunraven swept his gaze around the group. "We'll see you all back at the academy."

Then he and Cricklewood stepped through the gateway. And the window to safety, to our soft beds and new lives, snapped shut.

The walkers vanished immediately after the teachers, sprinting into the forest.

So much for interspecies cooperation.

I noted the direction they took. That was something at least.

Unless they'd known we'd be watching and chosen to deceive.

Ameline gripped my arm. "I don't think we should be splitting up."

I switched my attention back to the students I could still see. A few groups were being formed, and a cluster of guys with more daring than sense were stepping into the trees.

I raised my voice. It's not like the monsters didn't already know we were here.

"We'll be stronger if we all stick together."

The leader of the macho group scowled. "I'm not scared. And I'm not going to be the one swimming around that freezing lake."

I inhaled deeply and counted to three. "I didn't say you were scared. I'm saying your skills might benefit the rest of the group."

He looked unconvinced, and in desperation, I gestured at Ameline. "Like maybe *others* are scared and would be really grateful if you stuck around to help."

I felt Ameline shrink at the unwanted attention and whispered an apology.

"It's all right," she murmured. "They might be idiots, but they don't deserve to die for it."

The macho guys were drifting back to the rest of us now, drawn in by the fantasy of rescuing pretty damsels in distress. It was a stereotype I was loath to propagate but one that came in handy right then.

The other half-formed groups seemed to recognize the wisdom of safety in numbers and stayed put. Good.

That was when I realized that not *all* the walkers had sprinted off.

Two had stayed behind.

As much as it galled me, I knew they were our best chance of making it back to the manor without casualties.

So I swallowed my pride, approached the nearest one, and forced my hand forward. I almost managed to keep it from trembling. "I'm Nova. Who are you?"

It was not the question I wanted to ask. Not even in the top ten.

He frowned at my proffered hand for a second—just long enough for me to realize the custom might not transcend species—then extended his own.

"Call me Theus."

His hand was warm and, to my surprise, callused. His grasp firm but with nothing to prove. If it hadn't been for his momentary confusion and his too-perfect beauty, I wouldn't have been able to tell the hand I'd just shaken was a walker's.

And boy was that beauty even more striking up close. His face was open and appealing, with clear-cut features, dark expressive eyebrows, and the faintest smattering of freckles. He was just a couple of inches taller than me, giving me a direct line of sight into his moss-green eyes—so like the forest that they drew me into their depths.

I stepped back.

"Slow runner, Theus?" I inquired casually.

His perfect brow furrowed. "Sorry?"

I waved a hand at the students, most of them huddled together like sheep waiting for the big bad wolf to come and get them.

"You stayed behind while the others ran. There are only two ways to get points in this trial. Speed, or acting as savior to the poor helpless humans."

"Oh. Right." He glanced at the second walker, who'd remained behind. She was the frost-haired girl from my Warfare Strategies class, and she was ignoring us all, crouching over a trio of toadstools like they might hold the meaning to life.

"That's Lirielle," Theus said. "Her mind works differently than most, but it's sharp enough, and she's lethal in a fight."

I'll bet she was.

The girl rose with liquid speed and snapped her attention to us. "I will stand with you, prophesied one."

Caught in the strange intensity of her smoky blue gaze, for a surreal moment I thought she was talking to me.

Then Theus said thank you, and I felt like an idiot.

I glanced from her lovely, delicate features to his. "Prophesied one?"

Theus shrugged uncomfortably. "Just some old thing no one really understands. Lirielle is... *unique* in thinking that it has anything to do with me."

The way he'd said *unique* suggested he'd wanted to say *wrong*.

Right now I didn't care.

I brushed my dagger hilt through the hole I'd put in my pants pocket and the thaumaturgy rod I barely knew how to use. Not convinced either of them would save us from the creatures roaming the woods. Not convinced I could trust the walkers to save us either.

But it was still the best shot we had.

"Okay, prophesied one"—I smirked to cover my fear—"how do we get everyone back to the academy alive?"

# CHAPTER 12

The answer, of course, was with great difficulty.

It was a miracle we weren't attacked in the long minutes it took to organize ourselves. Perhaps the teachers had somehow protected the clearing.

Perhaps we should stay there until they came to fetch us in disgust.

Or perhaps they'd let us die.

One thing was certain; none of us would be getting any points for speed.

Eventually Theus and Lirielle took the lead while Bryn, Ameline, Klay, and I formed the rearguard.

Bryn and Klay had both been first to light the candle in their respective magic classes, and I wasn't letting Ameline out of my sight.

We crept out of the clearing, almost as slow as the snails Cricklewood had accused us of being. We'd gone three paces when I saw something move.

A raven maybe? They were one of the native species wily enough to thrive since the invasion. There was plenty of food for scavengers after all.

Stories said they would flock to the site of an oncoming battle as if they could sense a feast was imminent. Many cultures had considered them dark omens. Harbingers of death.

But was it just me or had that particular raven have antlers?

I didn't point it out to Ameline, whose hand was trembling hard enough around her wand. Bryn in contrast was looking more cheerful than I'd seen her all day. Like this was some grand adventure.

I shook my head and concentrated on my own hands. My own senses. Keeping every one of them alert for incoming danger.

But I didn't see the vine shoot from the canopy above and snake around a kid's neck. I was facing behind us, monitoring for signs of pursuit.

The sound of a scream cut short made me whirl.

He was suspended a foot above the forest floor, his eyes wide and bulging, his fingers clawing futilely against the thick, sinewy vine cutting off his air supply.

For three heartbeats, I was too shocked to react. Then I forced my wand hand upward and visualized the vine letting go.

It was sloppily done, hard to make my brain focus on the image I wanted with the nightmare unfolding before me. I longed to make the evil thing wither but sensed that would use more power.

I was not alone in my casting.

At least two dozen spells hit it at once, and the vine burst into flames, flew backward, turned purple (who knew what that was meant to do), let go of its victim, and finally recoiled into the canopy.

All eyes were on the body of the boy sprawled in the leaf litter.

Then one of his hands lifted to gingerly touch his neck, and he sat up.

Alive!

A ragged cheer went up from our group.

The boy was shaken, his hair restyled by the flames that had ignited above his head, his neck bruised from the vine's grip and bruised worse from being flung through the air along with it, but *alive*.

He climbed to his feet, and several kids ran to help him rejoin our ranks. No one said a word about the awful stench of burned hair. Our first altercation with the wilderness had been a success, and most kids were bolstered by the small win.

I kept my own thoughts to myself. That if the strangler vine been the nasty kind with thorns that sank into the victim's flesh, we would have killed the kid, trying to save him. We were lucky we hadn't anyway. And if I'd been alone and fallen victim to that strangler vine, I didn't think I would've had the presence of mind or the focus to save myself. Not with magic anyway. Who could summon the clear imagining needed to spellcast while being dragged off to be eaten?

Instead of lowering morale by voicing any of that, I retrieved my dagger from its sheath for faster access. Then worked with the group to organize a rotating system for who was on wand duty at any given time and spread them throughout the crowd. Hopefully the next crisis would be dealt with more efficiently. In part to waste less magic, and in part to reduce the likelihood of harming the person we were trying to save.

We set off once more, everyone on lookout duty now. We made it all of three hundred yards before the group jerked to a stop.

"We need to back up and go a different route," the green-eyed walker called from the front. "Tread lightly. There's a terrant nest ahead."

I swallowed. Professor Wilverness had taught us about terrants today. They were small but carnivorous ant-like insects that nested in the soil in huge numbers. I couldn't remember if it was magic or mechanics, but the evil critters hunted by shifting the soil out of their way to form a kind of terrant-filled quicksand beneath the leaf litter. Their unsuspecting prey would step into this trap and immediately be feasted upon by the millions upon millions of devouring insects.

Oh, and worst of all, they could *move* their quicksand deathtrap, following vibrations on the forest floor to capture their prey.

"Nobody move," I shouted back. "Theus, you

95

might've noticed we aren't as light on our feet as you walkers."

It was amazing the terrants weren't already moving toward us. Or maybe they were.

"Before anyone takes another step, we should use magic to kill them or hold them or—"

A tree branch crashed to the forest floor thirty feet to our right.

"Redirect them?" finished Theus.

Another tree branch fell, close to the first but a little farther away.

I hoped whatever lived in those trees wouldn't want revenge. Maybe it was just a nice, normal squirrel.

Sure. Why not?

A minute passed, and then another, and nothing came screeching from the treetops. Theus and Lirielle announced the way was clear, and the group moved forward again, giving the recently terrant-occupied ground an extra-wide berth.

We traveled what I estimated to be a mile without further incident. Perhaps Theus and Lirielle were doing something with their much stronger magic to keep the monsters at bay. Or maybe the teachers were doing more than they'd admitted to.

When nothing was trying to feast on your flesh, the forest was eerily beautiful. I'd had dreams, sometimes, of walking through it. But my dreams were nowhere near as good as the real thing.

I began to hope we'd make it.

Nor was I alone in that. Around me, my classmates were showing signs of relaxation. Lowered shoulders. Wands clutched less tightly. Gazes wide with wonder rather than worry.

Then Misty, an absentminded girl who I suspected might've been responsible for turning the strangler vine purple, gasped in delight.

"Look, it's a flum!"

She dashed over to the fluff ball of a creature, and contrary to what I expected, it didn't run from her advance.

I adjusted my grip on the dagger in my right hand and the wand in my left.

*Why* wasn't it running away? Her clueless approach ought to terrify a small prey animal. Was it injured? By a much meaner predator who was still lurking nearby perhaps?

Misty reached the flum and bent down to pet it or pick it up or something equally inadvisable.

"Don't!" Theus snapped from the front of our group.

Then the earth exploded.

Misty screamed.

Clods of dirt pelted me in the face.

And the flum vanished as a humongous, hulking brute twice the size of a grizzly bear erupted out of the soil.

The monster looked a lot like an overgrown groundhog except for its giant jaw crammed full of vicious, triangular teeth.

The kind of teeth that specialized in shredding flesh.

Misty had been flung back by the force of the monster's ascent and was crab crawling away still shrieking.

But the beast took only a fraction of a second to locate her. It lunged forward and down, its fearsome maw open wide.

There was no time for magic.

I hurled my dagger at the monster. It was like stabbing a grizzly with a toothpick, but maybe it would buy a few precious seconds.

My dagger lodged in the brute's eye. A lucky shot. I was good, but not that good.

The gaping maw recoiled and snapped shut. Then opened again to bellow so loud and deep I felt it thrum through my bones—along with a good dose of terror.

But by now some of the other kids had gathered their magic focus, and they blasted the monster back. It roared again in fury, but Misty was scrambling out of reach, and more magic pelted the beast.

Even so, it wasn't going anywhere. Our simple spells were no more than wasp stings. A painful nuisance, but the monster's outrage would soon overcome them.

Should I try a bigger, nastier spell and risk knocking myself out? Or worse?

That was when the walker Lirielle glided over to stand between the monster and its prey.

She was average height but slender, with a loveliness

that seemed too fragile for this world. And she was utterly dwarfed by the savage, snarling beast.

Despite myself, I felt a flash of fear for her.

Then she placed a dainty hand on her hip and spoke softly.

"Run, little one. I'll give you three seconds."

The monster dropped to all fours and shuffled back a step. Then another. Then, with a final bellow of frustration, it turned and loped away.

That was good.

What was less good was that the brute had stolen my dagger.

Misty staggered into the safety of the group and broke down in sobs. No doubt a mixture of delayed shock and fresh relief.

The nearest kids rubbed or patted her back, and after a minute, she wiped her eyes on her sleeve. "Wha... what happened to the... flum?"

Lirielle turned and canted her head at the girl as if in mild curiosity.

"There was no flum," she stated in her musical yet oddly inflectionless voice. "The groundbeast uses its tail as a lure to attract other predators, then bursts out of the earth and devours them."

"Oh," Misty managed.

"It is fortunate you did not sink your teeth into the lure like a predator would have, or you would have been eaten in return."

"Oh," Misty said again. But she'd stopped crying now.

Lirielle seemed to interpret this as a natural end to the conversation and drifted back to the head of the group. Klay and Bryn assigned new kids to spell-casting duty on the side of the attack, and our shell-shocked group trudged onward.

I had a bad feeling I would regret losing that dagger.

The next magical creature we came across was already dead.

Decapitated, to be precise.

It was a dragon. A massive, glittering dragon, twice again the size of the groundbeast, its copper scales undimmed by death. The sight of such a terrifying yet magnificent creature slain hit me harder than I expected.

The other walkers must have done this.

The idea that they could—and had—bested such a creature, that they'd cut off its head rather than evading it—was perhaps more frightening than the dragon itself. And though I was pleased we did not have to face the legendary beast, a part of me grieved at its passing.

Ameline too looked upon its body with regret.

Bryn went up and poked at its teeth. "These things are *huge*!" She glanced over at us. "Anyone know if the scales are worth something?"

When no one answered, she rolled her eyes, tugged fruitlessly at one of the beautiful, glimmering scales, and stalked back to take her place in the group.

Fifteen minutes of trudging later, the manicured

lawn of Millicent Manor could be spied through gaps in the forest's undergrowth. I could've cried in relief.

A few of the kids did.

But we weren't safe yet.

An eerie wail bounced off the trees, quickly followed by another, and another, until a whole chorus of yowls filled the air. So many voices. And whatever was responsible for making the racket had us surrounded.

Our handful of designated casters were not going to be enough this time.

"Everyone prepare to fight," I shouted above the din. "But hold off so we attack as one. Pass the word."

Ten seconds later, the chorus abruptly ceased.

The ensuing silence was heavy with dread.

And then a horde of six-legged beasts slunk from the trees. They were small but many, like fox-sized hyenas with glowing amber eyes and an extra set of legs for slashing. They outnumbered us a dozen to one.

Make that two dozen to one.

On my left, Ameline breathed a curse.

On my right, Bryn brandished her wand like she was itching to use it again and said almost cheerfully, "Well, it was nice knowing you."

The ground trembled as someone, surely one of the walkers, made a wall of earth rise around us in an impromptu defense. It stopped at a height just low enough for us to see over.

"Wait for it," Klay said loud enough for everyone to hear. "Target one beast at a time. And use the barest minimum of magic you can manage to get rid of them. Don't panic."

The jerk had the audacity to sound calm. I was glad for it.

Incredibly, everyone *was* holding off to attack as a united force.

Either that or they were frozen in terror.

The beasts circled, unperturbed by the new landscaping, and sized us up, searching for the weakest angle.

I shared a quick glance with Klay over Bryn's head, and we spoke as one. "Now!"

Savage growls and high-pitched yelps erupted as dozens of spells hit the beasts.

As I'd feared, our attack only drove the pack to strike. Sure, some fell or fled, but many, many more came at us. They snarled and morphed into speeding blurs, leaping and scrabbling up the dirt wall four times their height like it was nothing.

The only upside to their sheer numbers was that they couldn't *all* charge at once.

Beside me, Ameline's wand flicked rapidly from one to another, and wherever she pointed, the beasts turned and ran. Maybe her rapport with creatures was somehow helping her.

Bryn was using a slower and less subtle method of lighting their furry ears on fire. But at least it worked.

I was still rotating through spell tactics. One I set on fire, another I choked with a mouthful of leaves, another I slashed across the nose with a magical blade, a fourth I trapped one of its six paws in the earth, and a fifth I distracted with the intestines of its felled pack mate. Every method worked, but none of them were as efficient as Ameline's.

We couldn't cast fast enough. Every beast we felled was replaced by three more, and an increasing number were making it to the top of the wall.

We were about to be overwhelmed when the barricade grew spikes. It skewered the most recent wave of ascending beasts, buying us precious seconds. But the ones behind simply clambered up their pack mates' bodies.

Kids behind me began to drop like flies. Not from the predators but from the spells we were casting to keep them away.

At least I hoped that was the case since I didn't think any of the creatures that had breached the wall had survived for more than a few seconds.

I cast a fear spell, then a slashing one. All the while, Dunraven's guerrilla warfare tactics and all the ways we were failing to use them churned in the back of my head.

*Never let your enemy choose the battleground. Never attack a larger force head-on. In an open field, a smaller force loses all its advantages. If you are taken by surprise, retreat and regroup to strike in more favorable circumstances.*

"That's all very well, Dunraven," I muttered. "But

what do you do when you're outnumbered, taken by surprise, and can't retreat?"

More kids behind me dropped. Almost a third of our number now.

In a desperate and dangerous move, I thrust my wand at the wall and imagined the spikes growing another six inches.

A fresh wave of the beasts skewered themselves upon the extended spikes, and I swayed, suddenly exhausted.

I'd used too much power. I'd lost my damned dagger. And the beasts were still coming.

One of them leaped over the wall and latched onto one of the unconscious kids. I lunged, grabbed it by the ruff of its neck, and flung it at one of its pack mates.

Three more took its place. I cursed and lunged at the nearest, planning on grabbing it and repeating my move, but it spun and snapped at my hand. I wrenched my fingers back from bloodstained teeth and, for want of a better weapon, smacked the beast over the head with my wand.

Kids who'd been focused on casting spells shrieked and leaped out of the way now that the nasty, vicious brutes were on our side of the wall. Too scared to use their wands or do anything but dodge, occasionally treading on the unconscious.

Bryn joined me in wrestling the beasts, then Klay did too. They at least both had daggers.

What the hell were the walkers doing? It hadn't escaped my notice that a lot more kids on their side of the circle were still standing, but if they could slay freaking dragons, then surely they could do more than this lousy wall.

"Theus, Lirielle, *do* something!" I yelled. "Or we're going to have casualties back here."

I dived at a beast that had clawed its way up a screeching girl's back. Their bites were nasty enough, but if they went for our jugulars, they'd be fatal. I wrenched it off her and swung it at a second who'd chosen easier prey in one of the unconscious kids. Both beasts slammed into the wall.

One crumpled, the other used the barricade as a springboard to vault back at me, four of its six sets of claws aimed for my face.

I dodged and spun. One claw caught my uniform and raked a stinging line across my skin. The fiend whirled in midair to face me again, but I was ready this time and caught it upon its landing with a wand to the skull.

Hoping no walker witnessed the way I'd just used the bone of their ancestor, I spun again, expecting to find a fresh target. But only humans moved within our makeshift stronghold. I wiped sweat from my face and forced my trembling legs to straighten so I could look over the wall.

A minute earlier, the earth beyond had been bare but for leaf litter and the occasional shrub. Now it was a dense jungle of bramble canes. Hundreds of beasts were trapped inside, letting out little yips as they squirmed through the thorns to free themselves. Others had been impaled by the canes and would never move again. But in either case, they were no longer trying to get to us.

I turned to stare at Lirielle and Theus, unsure whether to thank or curse them. Why the hell hadn't they pulled out that little trick sooner?

A nearby moan drew my attention back to more important matters. Ameline and Bryn were both scratched up but still standing. The relief of that made my knees weak. Or maybe that was my bone-deep weariness.

But many of our classmates were not so lucky.

I wiped my hair out of my face with my least-bloody forearm. "Good work, everyone. We're almost safe. So whoever has the strength to help carry one of the knocked-out kids, now's the time."

Jayden was one of the still conscious—unfortunately. "I'm exhausted."

I glared at him. "We're *all* exhausted." I didn't mention the two obvious exceptions. "Suck it up. We're not leaving anyone behind."

No one else complained. Not even the burned-hair, half-strangled vine victim who looked barely able to carry himself.

With a third of our number down, it was going to be a long, hard slog to the academy. I just prayed we wouldn't be attacked along the way and that every one of those downed kids was merely unconscious.

I didn't have the heart to tell people to check.

Besides, even if they *were* dead, I didn't want to leave them here.

The walkers cleared a path through the brambles like Moses and the Red Sea and led us forward. Neither of them had broken a sweat.

The fact they were shoulder-carrying a couple of kids each made me less sour about that.

Three grueling minutes later, we collapsed on the lawn of Millicent Manor.

# CHAPTER 13

We were rewarded for our courage and teamwork...

With Cricklewood comparing our speed unfavorably to that of a lamed turtle's. Then promising us all extra laps the next day.

The real reward was simple.

Nobody died.

Dunraven handed out an antiseptic healing salve for smaller scrapes and cuts. The unconscious kids and those with more serious injuries were taken to the infirmary.

Once Ameline, Bryn, and I had recovered for a minute, we staggered our way up the steps of the manor and straight to the girls' bathroom.

I didn't have the strength to fight with Millicent for hot water, so Ameline filled a bucket for me, and I used that to wash away the sweat, grime, and blood.

Afterward we slathered ourselves in the healing salve and fell into our beds. I don't think I was asleep *before* my head touched my pillow. But I was dead to the world three seconds after.

I woke some hours later to the drumming thunder of rain and lashing wind that rattled the window in its frame. No light leaked around the curtain, so it was still dark outside.

My body was heavy with fatigue, but I forced myself to sit up.

I didn't think the intensity of our studies was going to lessen anytime soon. And I wasn't about to waste the three months I had here mindlessly following orders until… Well, whatever was coming after the trial phase occurred. Assuming any humans survived that long.

I needed answers. Needed to know what was really going on here. Why on earth were the walkers arming us with knowledge and wands when it was clear to everyone that humans were inferior in every way the walkers cared about? Why were we competing in a series of deadly trials just to earn the "right" to continue at the academy? And if at least *some* human students supposedly made it through this three-month trial period, where were all the kids from previous intakes?

My heart twisted in my chest the way it always did when I thought of Fletcher. The boy next door. The eldest of four brothers. The gentle giant who'd always been there when I needed him—whether that was getting me *in* or *out* of trouble.

If I'd had a second best friend growing up, Fletcher was it. Until two years ago when he'd stepped through that damn runegate. Vanishing from my life like all first-borns did to their families.

I'd been hoping ever since that I'd find him here.

I swung my feet out of bed. Somebody had to put an end to the Firstborn Agreement. *I* had to put an end to it. And if I was going to work toward that impossible goal, there was no time like the present.

Besides which, the noise of the storm would do an excellent job of covering any sounds I made snooping.

Millicent didn't light up the lamps on the walls as my feet touched the floorboards. Good. Better that Bryn and Ameline stay sleeping.

Bryn had stoked up the fire before collapsing into her own bed, so I could see enough in the warm glow of the embers to find my cloak, notebook, and wand. Lucky for me, Millicent hadn't made the door disappear either.

As soon as I'd slunk through, I imagined my wand emitting a faint light. I wasn't sure whether it'd work since I couldn't point the wand at itself. But just like that, I had myself a lantern of sorts.

As little as I liked the walkers, I had to admit their bones sure came in handy.

Now for the real test. Would Millicent rat me out? There was no one around to see her wallpaper gestures and she didn't seem to talk, but she *had* flipped me out of bed, so a sleeping teacher or golin wouldn't pose much of an obstacle. But *would* she rat me out? How much did she understand? Even if she knew enough to realize I was breaking some kind of rule, would she care? Or did she only care about damage to herself?

I remembered Grimwort's warning about setting the furniture on fire and decided I'd best avoid damaging anything she might consider hers in this snooping expedition.

Checking Dunraven's map, I headed for the nearest unmarked room. My bare feet were already turning cold against the floorboards, but I thought I might be appreciative of their stealth later, even with the lashing rain and howling wind as cover.

There was a visible door. That was a good start. The rooms I'd passed that had been marked as dormitories on the map hadn't been visible from the corridor, and I'd wondered whether my late-night exploration would be over before it began.

I tried the cool brass knob and felt a thrill of anticipation when it turned. Until it opened to an empty room. That explained why it was unlocked.

I moved to the next unmarked room and found an unused classroom, the chairs and tables collecting dust against the wall. The third room contained an assortment of long-dead plants. All right then. Interesting but not useful. The fourth doorknob I tried was locked.

If I hadn't drained my magic reserves to nil a few hours ago, I might have tried my wand. But caution made me reach for my dagger sheath. My dagger was gone of course, but the holder concealed a few other useful tools, including my set of lockpicks.

A local guy had made a study of locks so he could open doors, padlocks, and safes whose keys and owners had been lost in the invasion. I'd traded the information for chopping up a winter's worth of firewood and lugging a backbreaking amount of water. The result being that I knew how locks worked. Not that I had the gear on me to crack a complex safe right now.

But the old doorknob was no challenge—a simple pin tumbler lock that my tools made short work of.

I'd half expected it to eschew mundane locking mechanisms altogether for some kind of walker magic, but then Millicent had doubtless existed a long time before the walkers moved in. Not in *sentient* form of course, but the point remained.

Luckily for me.

Inside was someone's office. I closed the door behind me and checked my map again. If vicinity was any indication, it might have been Grimwort's office.

I grimaced. Best *not* to imagine what he'd do if he caught me snooping.

Wand light outstretched, I ventured deeper into the room. Bookshelves lined the back wall, but the titles I could see were all in foreign languages, and the shelves held as many trinkets as they did books. On my right were two matching wardrobes, and on the left was a generous rosewood desk. I moved toward the latter.

There were no drawers to rummage through, but the surface held a stack of the notebooks they'd provided us with, an oversized golden quill, the skull of a creature I didn't recognize, and a small iron chest.

I flicked open a few of the notebooks in case they'd belonged to a prior student, but the pages were blank. My gaze landed back on the small iron chest. It was intricately etched with a labyrinth of tiny, delicate leaves, but what caught my attention were the two locks that bound it shut.

One was of human make, a complex pick-resistant padlock with seven pins and an unusual, narrow keyway that would take a good five minutes and most of my skill to unlock. A different league altogether than the one on the door.

The second lock must have been magical in origin. A miniature dragon, impressively lifelike but made of solid steel, had its tail wrapped around the padlock loops. When I drew near, the dragon yawned, displaying rows of needle-sharp teeth, and opened violet eyes to regard me.

A violent gust of wind rattled the window and I jumped, unable to stop myself glancing around the room. No one was there. Of course.

Chiding myself, I turned back to the chest. I would focus on the magic lock first. If I couldn't convince the dragon to let me in, there was no point unlocking its mundane counterpart.

Experimentally I poked a pick inside the dragon's mouth to learn if it had any recognizable locking mechanisms. The tiny steel teeth chomped down and snapped the tool in two.

I snatched my hand away and cursed. I should've seen that coming. But at least I had other picks. Not that I'd be using them anywhere near the little monster's mouth.

Instead, I retrieved my wand light from the desk. "Okay, wandy, we've been through battle now, you and I, right? We're on the same team?"

My wand—or more accurately, the walker's bone I was borrowing—did not answer.

I aimed it at my quarry and visualized the miniature dragon unwinding its twining tail from the padlock loops.

The dragon snarled and spat a ball of flame at me. I didn't have time to dodge.

The tiny fireball hit my stomach, but our uniforms must've been burn-resistant as well as sweat, stain, and tear-resistant, because the flame died.

"Yikes." I patted the smoking spot on my shirt and chewed my lip in contemplation. "Okay, tough guy. Don't like being told what to do, is that it?"

Wilverness had said real dragons rarely deigned to cooperate with other beings.

"But I bet you must get hungry, sitting here guarding your treasure day in and day out?"

The dragon's eyes narrowed, but it didn't spit more flame, and I thought there might've been a flash of a tiny forked tongue across its teeth.

I'd conjured fire out of thin air. How hard could it be to conjure a chunk of raw meat?

Or would it only work if I conjured a miniature prey animal the dragon could chase around the room? If so, I might have to give up on unlocking this chest and return to bed. I doubted my power reservoir had refilled yet, and my feet were freezing.

So I pictured a cube of raw meat. Imagined the smell, the color, the texture (but not the taste) and aimed my wand just in front of the dragon.

Sure enough, a chunk of meat appeared, albeit a little smaller than I'd intended.

Wow.

No wonder the walkers hadn't given all humans wands like these. We wouldn't be dependent on them if we could conjure our own food.

Not that I knew whether magically created food had the nutritional value of the real thing. And maybe it wouldn't be sustainable even then, because I *felt* the energy leave my body. Either I hadn't recovered yet, or making something out of nothing was costly.

But the dragon's eyes widened and it made a little rumbling sound. Almost like it was purring. Then it unraveled its tail of its own accord and climbed down the chest for its midnight snack.

I was simultaneously delighted and dismayed. How much time had I just bought myself? Perhaps I should've picked the mundane padlock first after all.

I set to work. The narrow keyway made the

unpicking especially awkward, and I had to stop and recast the spell two more times before the greedy lizard curled up and went to sleep on the desk. But at last I got the chest unlocked.

Abruptly nervous, I took a steadying breath and opened the lid.

Inside the chest was a single object. An elegant ebony circlet resting on a pillow of green satin.

I tried to imagine Grimwort wearing it and snickered at the image.

So why was it here? Sure, it was pretty enough, but the walkers weren't short on jewels or riches. Why go to such lengths to protect it? Sentiment?

I brushed my fingers over its cool, polished surface and felt the sudden need to try it on. To wear it. Just for a second.

My hands moved before I'd finished processing the strange compulsion, and I placed the circlet on my head.

Darkness swallowed me.

It was not the darkness of night. It was less, and it was more. It was the absence of all. A nothingness so thick I could choke on it.

Fear squeezed my lungs, my throat, and yet I was no longer sure I had a body. That I had ever possessed a body. I waved my theoretical hand in front of my eyes and saw nothing. Not a stir. There was a metallic taste on my tongue. The pressure of the void heavy in my ears. If I indeed possessed either. And the fear.

That. *That* was real.

Real and growing. Rising. Building and ascending in some crashing, clamoring, monstrous crescendo I could not hear.

I couldn't breathe. Did not know if I needed to.

And then *it* came. I knew not what it was, only that it was hunting, ravenous. And coming for me.

I stumbled backward, unable to pant in fear for I had no breath to expel. My body, or my sense of such an odd construct, was being crushed under the weight of the darkness.

Then *something* brushed against the fingers I did not have. *Something* breathed hot, hungry breaths that pierced even the nothingness. And I stumbled backward another step, wishing with every fiber of my being that I could scream.

I fell instead. Smashing my head against timber. And the horrendous, terrifying blackness was replaced by the dark of night. Three paces away, my wand light still glowed. And by its illumination I had just enough time to see the circlet on the ground beside me before the wardrobe I'd apparently fallen into slammed shut.

I didn't even care. I sucked in greedy, panicked breaths, and the timber against my back became more solid. The pain in my oxygen-starved lungs and limbs more apparent.

Or maybe it was more than that. Every muscle ached and trembled. My mouth was bloody where I'd bitten my tongue. And it took long minutes for me to recollect myself.

I was in a wardrobe. In an office I'd broken into. With an evil circlet thing lying far too close for comfort.

I forced my trembling legs beneath me, shifted swathes of fabric aside to make room, and pushed myself into a standing position. It took a lot more steadying breaths before I could stop leaning against the wardrobe for support.

When I could stand unassisted, I shoved at the door.

It did not open.

I shoved harder, putting my shoulder into it.

The timber didn't so much as budge.

I groaned as realization set in.

Millicent had locked me in the cupboard with the circlet I was desperate to get away from so I would be caught for trespassing.

# CHAPTER 14

I'd somehow dropped both my wand and my lockpicks when the circlet had compelled me to wear it. And when I fumbled for a lock in the dark, I could find no mechanism to unpick regardless.

"This isn't funny, Millicent," I muttered. "Let me out."

The horror of... Well, whatever that had been was sticking to me like the world's worst spiderweb, and I wanted to get the hell out of this dark cupboard *now*.

Screw it then. I felt each side of the wardrobe, searching for the weakest component. The rear panel was the thinnest.

Hoping there was at least a small gap between the cupboard and the wall, I pressed my back against the stupid door that refused to open, and used the leverage to kick the rear panel with every bit of strength I could muster.

My heel went through with a satisfying crack, letting in a smidgen of the light I craved. I didn't even care that the noise might be audible over the pouring rain. I repeated the process a few more times until I could rip away large pieces of the splintered wood with my hands.

So much for not breaking anything.

I didn't know how much the manor understood, but just in case, I hissed, "For the record, Millicent, I wouldn't have damaged the wardrobe if you hadn't trapped me inside. This one's on you."

Somehow I didn't think she'd be swayed around to my way of thinking.

There were only a couple of inches between the wardrobe and the wall it sat against, but with persistence and a great deal of shoving and wriggling, I managed to shift my temporary prison far enough to enable my escape.

I squirmed out of the jagged hole I'd created, shuffled sideways around the wardrobe, and returned at last to the rosewood desk where it had all begun. Thank every saint of thieves and snooping. Despite the exertion, my breaths came easier out here.

But I didn't have time to linger. Someone might've heard me, and if not, Millicent might be mad enough to throw a professor out of bed.

I retrieved my wand and lockpicks, then did a quick survey of the room. For bonus points, breaking out the *back* of the cupboard meant whoever this office belonged to—aside from Millicent herself—might fail to realize what I'd done. For a while at least.

I was so exhausted a magical repair attempt was out of the question. It was a miracle my wand was still glowing.

But if I wanted a chance of my break-in going unnoticed, that open, empty iron chest was another matter entirely.

My heart started galloping like a three-legged horse. The circlet. I had to return it.

I groaned. I didn't want to so much as go near it again. There was no damn way I was about to touch it.

So I selected a book from the shelf, slid my wand into my belt clip, and returned reluctantly to the wardrobe. On the off chance it had unjammed itself since my escape, I tried the door first. It swung open without resistance.

Relief and annoyance fought for dominance. I chose gratitude. A wary kind of gratitude in case Millicent was planning to smack me with the door that just opened, but still. It wasn't like I couldn't escape a second time. And it would be a lot easier to remove the circlet without accidentally touching it this way.

The evil thing was still where it'd landed—thrown from my head as I'd fallen backward into the wardrobe. Even looking at it made me uncomfortable, so I averted my gaze and clasped it between the pages of the book.

Hands outstretched, I carried it gingerly over to the waiting chest, dropped it inside, and shut the etched iron lid. The miniature dragon climbed up the case and wrapped his tail around the padlock loops before returning to what seemed like ordinary, lifeless steel.

My shoulders relaxed a fraction. But if someone was coming for me, I wasn't sticking around to greet them.

I snapped the second lock into place, shuffled the hangers in the wardrobe to hide the gaping hole, and shoved the whole thing back into place against the wall. A final glance around the office didn't reveal any obvious signs of my intrusion except for my map of Millicent, which I grabbed. It would have to do.

Fatigue pulled at me as I slipped from the room, urging me toward my bed. I felt less horrible than when I'd first been released from the circlet's power, but that wasn't saying much.

Besides, Millicent clearly *did* care if I was snooping. Or her grudge meant she wanted to thwart me at every turn regardless. Either way, I wasn't going to get far unless I could convince her we'd just gotten off on the wrong foot.

But coming up with a way to reconcile with a sentient building was beyond my current abilities. So I gave up fighting the fatigue and headed for my dorm room.

Which was when Theus found me.

He'd been walking through the halls without the aid of a light, which would've made it easy to spot mine. Darn walkers and their superior everythings. And when I turned down a junction of the corridor, there he was.

My overwrought heart started galloping again. Did he know what I was up to? Would he throw me to the wolves (or the professors—which might be worse) if he did?

How could I explain my presence? The bathroom was in the opposite direction, so that explanation was out. Unless he'd believe I was stupid enough to forget.

Yeah, that might work.

Except my notebook was still open to Dunraven's map. And who knew what state of dishevelment I was in after the dragon flame, the circlet, and the wardrobe?

He, on the other hand, was just as striking as I remembered. His only concession to the late hour being his chestnut hair that was slightly more unruly than usual.

Then my instincts kicked into gear, alerting me I was in the vicinity of a *predator,* and my mind went racing off in another direction.

What if the academy ruse was just an odd game they liked to play before they ate us? Or a distraction to keep the livestock from panicking while they picked us off one by one? After all, chronic terror couldn't do good things for the quality of one's meat supply.

And if we *were* here to be slowly consumed, what better place to single one out from the herd than in the middle of the night with the storm to cover my screams?

But Theus did not attack me. Nor did he threaten to call the teachers. Though I couldn't rule out the possibility he'd done so through magical means beyond my ability to sense.

Instead, he said, "You're the girl from the trial. The one that saved the flum kid with quick thinking and an impressive throw. Nova, right?"

I wet my lips, uncertain whether him remembering me was good or bad.

"That's me." The words came out a smidgen higher than I'd have preferred. "And you're the one that saved all of us. *Eventually.*" I couldn't help but amend.

Then I remembered my resolution to play nice—but not *too* nice with the pretty walkers, and added, "Hope the points were worth it."

His eyes crinkled, but he didn't elect to comment. "What are you looking for?" he asked instead.

I had the distinct feeling that answering *my bed* wouldn't cut it. So I lifted my chin. Why should I bother hiding the truth? Or at least part of the truth. I wasn't the one in the wrong here.

"I wanted to find the firstborns that came here in previous years."

All of them, but one in particular.

Theus went against my expectations by offering me information. Sort of.

"They're not here."

"Then where are they?"

"It's not my place to say."

I clamped down my frustration. Why the hell was everybody at this academy so damn secretive? What were they afraid we'd find out? Or do with that knowledge?

I reframed the frustration in my mind. If they were secretive, they had something to hide. And if they bothered to hide it from the pathetic humans, then logic suggested the walkers must be vulnerable. Somewhere. Somehow. A vulnerability I might one day exploit.

If I played my cards right.

So I allowed Theus to evade that question and asked instead, "Are they alive?"

"Most of them."

The lack of hesitation in his answer gave me some small measure of hope. Then he murmured something I didn't quite catch, something that sounded like "sort of," and I tried to clamp down on hope too.

Still, this walker seemed to have more time for humans than the others. Plus he was polite enough not to comment on my unkempt state. Either that or he hadn't noticed—maybe the comparative imperfection of human features always looked messy to walkers.

But even if he'd been as condescending as the rest of them, the undeniable truth was that without his and Lirielle's aid in yesterday's trial, many of us would've been killed.

"Why'd you do it?" I found myself asking.

"Do what?"

I shrugged, trying to pretend the answer didn't matter so much. "I don't know. Save us in the trial. But not until the last possible minute."

*After we'd pushed ourselves to the breaking point, protecting ourselves with unfamiliar magic, and a full third of our number had passed out.*

"How much do you know about world walker culture?" he asked.

"Around as much as I know about the mating rituals of unicorns."

Theus looked puzzled. "Do you know a lot about the mating rituals of unicorns?"

The joke had gone straight over his head, but somehow *I* was the one blushing.

"No, nothing!"

He seemed to accept that. "All right. In walker culture, honor and strength are paramount. They're valued far above trivial, transient things like fear or risk, and it's considered humiliating to be so weak as to require rescue. Which is why I didn't want to step in unless I had to."

He studied me for a moment, his deep green eyes unreadable. "Or until you asked."

Until I *asked?*

*Really?*

I recalled that desperate fight inside our increasingly overrun dirt walls. The air thick with blood, my limbs heavy with exhaustion, and the dread that seized my chest as I'd realized in a horrid moment of clarity that some of the kids around me were going to die.

Unless the walkers intervened.

I'd *asked* all right. In desperation, I'd cried out for help that I wasn't sure would come.

And in the present, I managed—barely—to restrain myself from throttling Theus.

"Besides," he continued after I failed to muster an appropriate response, "swarmcats are relatively nonlethal compared to most of what the students are going to be facing here. It's best that the first time you bloody your blade—or wand in this case—you do so against an easy foe. They'll be grateful for it later."

That at least made a disturbing sort of sense. One that didn't leave me with any warm fuzzies about the upcoming trials.

"But I saw you fight. You would have survived even when not everyone else did."

He said this like it was supposed to make me feel better. And the ludicrousness of that finally got my tongue to work.

"That doesn't make it okay."

He looked at me without comprehension. Or maybe I just couldn't read him.

"All your questions are about the welfare of strangers," he said. "From what I was taught of human sentiment, I thought you would be more concerned about your family."

I stared back at that beautiful face, equally uncomprehending. How could this be difficult to understand?

"It's not an either-or proposition," I pointed out. "I

love my family and would give anything to see them again, but that doesn't mean I can't care about strangers."

If he couldn't grasp why it mattered to me if kids died at my side, I didn't feel like explaining it to him.

But he went against my expectations a second time.

"I could allow you to see them—your family—through a visual gateway, if you like?"

"You could?" The words slipped out before suspicion overcame me. "Why would you do that?"

He shrugged, an oddly elegant gesture on a walker.

"Because it is my understanding that humans place more importance on family ties than walkers do. Because it will cost me little and may mean a great deal to you."

"What do you want in return?"

He smiled faintly. "For you to look at me with less suspicion when I'm trying to help you would be nice. But you will owe me nothing. Not even that."

I bit my tongue on my next words. *Why then? Why would you do me this kindness when your kind have done nothing but harm to mine?*

I was here to learn. Here to play along. To play nice. Until I'd gleaned enough information to formulate a plan and execute it. And if I wanted more information than the crumbs they fed us, I needed a "friend" among the walkers. They kept their secrets close to their chests. Which meant the only way to learn them was to get close too.

And if it was a trap? How better to determine the

nature of your hunter than to follow him meekly into the snare and let him tighten it around your neck?

By watching what happened when he laid it around someone else's neck, I supposed.

But I was the only one here.

And the lure he'd placed in the trap was well chosen.

So I nodded and said, "Then I would like that very much."

# CHAPTER 15

The "hunter" led me to the girls' bathroom.

Okay, that was sort of weird. But either Theus was taking me somewhere it would be easier to clean up the blood, or he needed a mirror as he claimed.

I was about to find out which.

"Why the *girls'* bathroom?"

"They're cleaner. Trust me."

"And you really need a mirror for this? I mean, you can walk across worlds and open gateways with a wave of your hand, but you need a freaking enchanted mirror like in *Beauty and the Beast*?"

He shrugged. "I'm not sure what *Beauty and the Beast* is, but any ordinary mirror will do. And if we weren't inside this particular manor, I wouldn't need one of those either."

I wondered if that might prove important one day. "What's different?"

"Gateway magic is protected against inside these walls. Only the professors have the override."

That was good to know. If you took out the teachers and staged a coup, the manor could be used as a stronghold. One where the walkers couldn't just use their magic to appear behind you and slit your throat.

I hoped Theus wasn't being so open with me because he was about to slit mine.

We pushed through the bathroom door, and Millicent lit up the room. Maybe she was pretending to be good in front of the walker.

He went straight to the nearest mirror.

"A former student figured out the mirrors are a sort of loophole. Or a form of gateway magic the professors didn't bother to ward against. It allows us to see out but no more than that."

I trailed up behind him, and our eyes met in the reflection. It felt strangely intimate.

Then he pulled out a knife.

"I'll need some of your blood as a link to your family, otherwise we'll spend all night trying to locate them."

As soon as I'd recovered from my minor heart attack, I snatched the knife from him. It wouldn't take much to reopen the latest Millicent bite on my finger. But come on, what was with this place and everything needing blood?

What I asked aloud was, "Where do you want it?"

"On the mirror."

I smeared my bleeding finger on the glass. Would the magic drink it like Millicent seemed to? Or would I have to clean it up when we were done?

Theus concentrated on the bloody smear and placed his palm against the mirror beside it.

Then I forgot all about Theus.

Because there in front of me, almost life-sized, were my brother and sister.

Reuben's face was serene in sleep, stripped of the attitude he displayed during the day. And though he was going through the phase where he was too cool and tough to hang out with his little sister in public, there was Mila curled up beside him.

Actually, *curled up* was a misleading description. She might be little, but she was a chronic bed hog.

My back had borne testament to that many a time after I'd wound up sleeping awkwardly over the edge of the mattress to accommodate her sprawling limbs. And it looked like poor Reuben's back would pay the same price come morning.

I smiled so hard my teeth hurt.

Mila too looked serene in sleep, though a smudge of dirt under her chin suggested she hadn't changed her daytime behavior any more than Reuben likely had.

The last handkerchief I'd given her was clutched tight in one small fist.

How could seeing them simultaneously hurt so much and yet fill the hollow ache in my chest I'd been carrying ever since I'd left them behind on that rooftop?

I stared at them. I don't know how long, drinking in every detail.

And then their beloved figures faded back into an ordinary mirror.

A mirror that showed far too clearly that I'd been crying. I hadn't noticed. And Theus had been standing right there, watching me cry.

Dammit.

I swiped my eyes and faced him in the flesh instead of the reflection. "Thank you. That did mean a great deal to me."

And perhaps because I'd so recently been staring at two of the people I loved most in the world, for a moment I saw Theus differently. Saw him as I might have had the invasion never happened and he'd been just a boy I met on the street.

I wasn't the swooning type, but damn, he was beautiful. Maybe not by walker standards, but I liked him more for his tiny imperfections. The unruly hair that never sat quite right. The freckles that dotted the bridge of his nose and scattered across his cheeks. The eyes that were not the brilliant, glittering green of other walkers but a deeper, richer shade, exquisitely framed by his dark lashes.

And through that temporary lens, I could've sworn I saw sadness and understanding in those eyes.

If my life had been my own, and if he had been human, I knew with utter certainty that I could have loved the young man before me.

But my life wasn't.

And he wasn't.

Not even close.

Exhaustion—both emotional and physical—hit me like a felled tree.

I headed for my dorm room.

Theus kept pace beside me but did not feel the need to fill the silence between us. Something I appreciated more than usual as I tried to hold on to that idyllic, heartwarming image of my sleeping siblings with everything I had.

Ugh, another reason to feel grateful to a walker.

It was only when I reached the red serpent that guarded my room that a new thought entered my sluggish brain. "Could you show me someone else?"

I was thinking of Fletcher. What I wouldn't give to see his face and know that he too was okay.

Theus's lips twitched. "Some other time maybe."

I nodded, not about to argue when I was already swaying on my feet. "Okay. Well, thanks again. Good night, Theus."

"Good night, Nova."

I watched him glide silently down the corridor into the darkness and then pressed my fingers to the wallpaper.

Millicent bit me *extra* hard before letting me inside.

# CHAPTER 16

I'd thought I'd gotten away with the night's snooping.

I was wrong.

I'd also expected to wake up face-first on the floor with my mattress on top of me after the wardrobe incident. But I was wrong about that too.

Ameline beat Millicent to it.

"Where the heck were you last night?" she demanded, concern etching her features. "I woke up and you were gone. And when I tried to go looking for you, Millicent wouldn't let me out."

I thought about that for a moment and figured it must have been when Millicent had me locked up and wanted to prevent anyone coming to my rescue.

Or maybe she just wanted to prevent her favorite Ameline from getting into trouble.

"Um. I went to the bathroom?" I tried—not sounding the least bit convincing.

It was way too early for an interrogation.

Ameline crossed her arms. "I waited up for you. For ages. But you were gone so long I must've fallen asleep."

By now, Bryn was stirring from her own slumber. She sat up, rubbing her eyes and making no attempt to pretend she wasn't listening with avid interest.

"Out with it," Ameline ordered. "*All* of it."

Bryn smirked. "Yes, I'd like to hear it too."

People often mistook Ameline's softness for weakness. I knew better. She might be sweet-natured and amiable about most things, but once she drew a line in the sand, so help you if you crossed it.

I could see by the set of her jaw that this was one of those times. So I told them.

The set of Ameline's jaw did not improve throughout my tale. Meanwhile, Bryn was all but bouncing on her bed—especially when I described breaking my way into the locked chest.

When I'd finished, Ameline gave me a dark look. "We're supposed to be in this together. You could've been hurt!"

"Yes," Bryn added, "and if you're going to go on fun life-endangering adventures in the middle of the night, the polite thing to do would be to invite us along."

Ameline's gaze flitted to Bryn—something I was grateful for just then.

"Um, well, missing out on fun wasn't exactly what I was afraid of, but I suppose the end result is the same."

Her gaze returned to me.

"You're not to go sneaking off alone again. You either cease your nighttime activities, or you take us with you."

The stubborn set of Ameline's jaw was still there, and Bryn was throwing her knife, spinning it into the air and catching it again, hilt first. Perhaps to signal she'd be a useful companion on a late-night jaunt. Or because she had trouble sitting still.

Either way, it was obvious they weren't about to take no for an answer.

I wanted to protect Ameline. *Needed* to protect her. But maybe in this case, that meant bringing her along.

The first trial proved we were stronger together. It also proved that the danger Dunraven had warned us about was real. And since no one would tell us what happened to those who failed the three-month trial phase, we *had* to be among the students that passed. Both of us. Because the thought of one of us continuing at the academy and the other...

Well, separation was not an option.

That meant any advantage, any edge, any foreknowledge our snooping might reveal, we needed. Not just for the first three months but for whatever came afterward too.

Even so, I made one last attempt to dissuade them. Or Ameline at least.

"You would have to break a lot of rules," I pointed out. "You hate breaking rules."

She scowled at me like she knew exactly what I was trying to do. She probably did.

"Nice try. But they threw the rulebook out the window when they magicked us into the middle of the freaking forest and told us to find our way home. Besides, they haven't explicitly forbidden us from exploring the manor."

Hmm. That was a good point. I wasn't sure they'd forbidden us from *anything* actually. Except making Grimwort repeat himself.

"Fine," I said. "Next time I go snooping, I'll take you with me."

Triumph flashed across both their faces.

"But before we try again, we need to work out a way of winning over Millicent."

Bryn snorted. "Why bother? If she wants to hold a grudge, let her. We can handle it."

Ameline shook her head. "Weren't you listening? She almost got Nova into serious trouble. Besides, do you really want cold showers the entire time you're here?"

Bryn missed the catch, and her dagger thudded blade-first into the floor.

Ameline snatched it up. "We're trying to win the manor over, not infuriate her further."

"All right, all right." Bryn conceded. She returned her butt to the mattress.

Or tried to. But the whole bed scooted out of the way so she landed on the floor. Right next to where the blade had bitten into the wood.

I bit back a snicker.

Ameline, who was, as ever, a better person than me, got straight back to the business at hand.

"Okay. So Millicent got mad at you for damaging her walls. Maybe fixing or restoring something for her will work. Have you noticed anything in bad shape?"

I grimaced.

"I might have destroyed the back of a wardrobe last night." I'd neglected to mention *that* detail in my retelling. "But only because she locked me inside."

Ameline pursed her lips. "I don't think repairing something you broke will go far in winning her over, but it might make her less mad at you at least. What else?"

She gave both Bryn and me a dirty look. "Something one of you *aren't* personally responsible for breaking."

I thought my way around the manor—or the parts of it we'd been to. "It's not broken exactly, but the stair-well by the dining hall has very creaky steps. Maybe we could tighten them up?"

Ameline rewarded me with a smile. "Good idea. We'll do it tonight then."

"Tonight," Bryn and I agreed.

And then we prepared ourselves for another morning of being tortured by Cricklewood.

# CHAPTER 17

That day's classes were more of the same, only worse.

The storm had tempered, but it was still raining hard while we ran around being yelled at by Cricklewood. That combined with our lingering exhaustion from the trial and the shell shock from everything we'd learned the day before meant it was a muddy, wet, and grueling two hours.

One kid sat down and refused to get up. Cricklewood didn't bother to argue. He simply plucked one of the long hairs from his chin, and the horrid thing grew and morphed into a gray whip that chased the rebel around and thwacked him soundly anytime he dared to slow.

I was so appalled I ran into one of the sentinel hedge cats, which rustled its leaves and hissed.

The sole highlight was that Cricklewood *didn't* promise to see us again that evening.

Maybe they wouldn't give us trials every day. A smart move if they wanted any of us humans to survive.

Then again, it was even odds they didn't.

I dragged myself from one classroom to the next, trying to cram my head with information while simultaneously wondering whether our plan to win over Millicent would work.

All right. And sometimes my thoughts drifted to Theus.

What were his motives for helping the humans? The trial I could understand since it was one of the ways to get points. But last night? No one had been around to assess him then, and I could think of nothing he might've derived from showing me my family.

So why offer?

*Because it will cost me little and may mean a great deal to you,* he'd said. And then claimed he'd wanted nothing in return. Like he was doing it out of pure benevolence.

I didn't believe that. Not for a second.

The Firstborn Agreement—the reason I was here right now—proved that the walkers didn't do anything for free. Let alone the way they'd rocked up fifty years ago on our world's metaphorical doorstep and demanded we accommodate them. Then proceeded to destroy most of the planet when we didn't respond the way they wanted.

So why then? Could Theus have his own agenda for gaining my trust? The way I hoped to gain his?

He'd been so much on my mind that when I walked

into my Rudimentary Magic class and saw him seated there, my first instinct was to pretend I hadn't. Last night he'd watched me cry. Seen my heart wide open as I'd looked at my siblings. He'd seen me vulnerable. And in the light of day, that felt acutely uncomfortable.

But regardless of *his* agenda, I needed him for my own. I couldn't afford to alienate him. So I waved a greeting and received a tug of a smile in response.

Was he amused by me or being friendly?

Grimwort stood up, and I switched my attention to the lesson. We had to direct a droplet of water through a series of small obstacles on our desks—without allowing its surface tension to break. It was a delicate task requiring oodles of finesse we didn't have, and every time my focus wavered, the droplet would burst and scatter in every direction. At which point I had to go through the painstaking process of re-forming it before starting over.

Under other circumstances, I might've enjoyed the challenge. But our lives were on the line, and it was difficult to see how this would help us survive the next trial.

Grimwort insisted superior concentration and self-control led to superior magic, then napped behind his desk for the rest of the lesson.

I exerted a great deal of self-control in not setting his chair on fire.

But I supposed I should've been grateful he wasn't accusing me of breaking into his office.

The walkers, of course, did not bother with the

exercise. Between the frustrating attempts with my water droplet, I noticed that with the exception of Lirielle, they largely ignored Theus. Almost as if he were beneath them the way they believed humans to be.

Was that because Theus was consorting with the livestock? Or some other inscrutable reason? He'd said honor and strength were of utmost importance in their culture. Had Theus somehow lost his?

I was concentrating on floating my water droplet through a paper tube when Lirielle drifted over to my desk.

"Beware," she said without inflection. Her smoky blue eyes fixed on mine with an intensity that mismatched her languid, dreamy manner. "The silent stares will bring you grief."

"Excuse me?"

She frowned. "The offense is not mine to excuse." Then she drifted away again without clarifying squat.

I glanced around. No one in the class was staring at me. I tried for half a minute to decipher the meaning behind her cryptic words, decided that way lay madness, and returned my attention to the water droplet.

That walker girl was *not* normal.

---

Bryn, Ameline, and I made it through the rest of our lessons, crammed in three extra hours of study and wand practice after dinner, then finally allowed ourselves to tackle the Millicent problem.

We all agreed that our first priority had to be our performance in class and the trials. As much as we wanted to uncover the truth behind this academy, it would do us no good if we failed the trial phase. Or worse, failed to *survive* the trial phase. So we'd settled on:

Survival first.

Passing second.

Snooping third.

The corridors were quiet, but it was still early enough they weren't entirely empty. It didn't matter. There was no need for stealth since no one could object to our *fixing* the stairs.

I held my wand over the bottom step of the ancient timber staircase and realized the flaw in our plan.

I had no idea how to go about this.

Pursing my lips, I walked the span of the step to find the creakiest point, aimed my wand, focused my imagination and will, and shifted my weight.

The timber groaned beneath me.

Well, I shouldn't have expected winning Millicent over would be easy.

I suspected she'd enjoy seeing me grovel, and I needed to get a better look at the step, so I got down on my hands and knees. Then gave up on that and lay flat against the floor.

It was going to be embarrassing if anyone walked past right now.

"If you're that tired, you really ought to go to bed," Bryn suggested sweetly from the top of the stairs.

She'd started at the other end, and I assumed by her lack of boasting that she wasn't having any better luck than me.

"I'd be less tired if you didn't snore like a pig choking on a donkey," I retorted. Actually, when she snored, she sounded almost dainty. But she didn't need to know that.

I wriggled until I was eye level with the step. "Ameline, walk up and down over this a few times, would you?"

Given she was already in Millicent's good books, Ameline had a supervisory role.

She obliged, and I saw the timber sag beneath her boot, shifting against the supports with an ominous groan. So I pointed my wand again and imagined the timber tread strengthening, visualizing it becoming as unyielding as stone so it would not bend or shift.

"Try again."

Ameline came down again, and this time the last step didn't make a peep when it bore her weight.

"Ha!" I crowed.

I had to take my victories where I could get them.

Bryn cheerfully lowered herself to my level, and with Ameline as our tester, we completed the whole staircase in about ten minutes.

I didn't know how long the magical strengthening would last. But I supposed if it wore off, we could always do it again.

Now to learn whether Millicent accepted our peace offering...

I was dusting myself off—already daydreaming about being woken by a gently rocking mattress rather than flung to the floor—when Glenn and Glennys came trotting up the staircase.

They got about a third of the way before their expressions changed. Not to one of pleasant surprise at the newly silent stairs. No. It was a look of horror.

One that quickly changed to pity on Glennys's face and a smirk on Glenn's. If you've never seen a golin smirk, count yourself lucky.

"What have you done?" Glenn asked.

"And more importantly, can you undo it?" Glennys added.

"Um," I said.

Ameline jumped in. "Nova and Bryn wanted to do something nice for Millicent. You know, after the, ahem, wall incident?"

Bryn crossed her arms. "We fixed the noisy old stairs for her. Why on earth would we undo it?"

Glenn's smirk widened into something more disturbing—though it was probably still supposed to be in the range of a smile. My supposition was confirmed a moment later when he did the braying laughter thing.

"Oh, you poor dears," Glennys said. "I'm afraid

you've just upset her further. Millicent *likes* her stairs and floorboards to be creaky. It's the closest thing to an audible voice she has, you see. She uses them to express herself."

Glenn paused his guffawing to explain. "Think about it like trying to apologize to someone by stuffing your dirty magical sock in their mouth."

I looked down at the golin's bare, clawed feet. What would they know about socks?

Unfortunately, they knew plenty about Millicent.

I groaned. Then groaned again when for some reason Lirielle's warning popped into my head, and this time it made sense.

*Beware, the silent stairs will bring you grief,* she'd said. I'd thought she'd meant *stares* and totally missed the point.

The walker girl might not be normal.

But that didn't mean she was wrong.

# CHAPTER 18

Two entire weeks passed by in a blur of lessons and practice and very little sleep.

Undoing our magic on the stairs had proven harder
than applying it in the first place, but thanks to
Ameline, the whole fiasco hadn't been a complete waste.
She'd had the presence of mind to ask the golin what
Millicent might accept by way of apology, and Glennys
had told us she liked gifts.

Not that we'd had any time to action the knowledge.
We were spending every spare moment cramming more
information into our heads or practicing our magic exercises until we'd drained our power reservoirs dry. And we
weren't the only ones.

Despite the difficulties of this odd magic school with
its side dish of death—the homesickness, the constant
fear of the next trial, living alongside the monsters who'd
destroyed our world, and suddenly being able to

perform magic—most kids had adapted surprisingly well to their new lives.

Perhaps in part because they were too exhausted to question the purpose behind it all, and I wondered if it had been planned that way. But humans are good at acclimatizing. If you live in constant fear and exhaustion, you get used to it. The emotions lose their edge, and you keep going because that's what has to be done.

So the second trial when it came was easier than the first. We were a little less incompetent, a little less unnerved, and this time each human was paired with a walker.

No one made any friends, but with the walkers' success dependent on keeping their human partner alive, no one died either.

Jayden came the closest when his inattentive walker had gotten distracted and forgot for a moment that Jayden existed.

The trial acted as a sort of wake-up call for Ameline, Bryn, and me. Yes, surviving and passing had to take precedence over snooping, but if we weren't careful, the three months would come to an end before we'd even managed to win over Millicent.

So that evening, given we were too exhausted for study anyway, we came up with a new plan.

"What kind of gifts might a building like?" I wondered aloud.

We were sitting around the fire that Bryn had made way too hot as usual, and I was beginning to sweat.

Ameline kicked me. "She doesn't like to be called that, remember?"

I bit back my first response. "Sorry, Millicent."

Not that verbal apologies had done me any good in the past. Still. That was why we were having this conversation.

"A piece of furniture?" Ameline suggested. "A pet? A nice non-hazardous plant?"

Bryn, who never seemed to get too hot, was sprawled out on the floor in front of the fire. "Maybe she likes jewels or other valuables. Pretty trinkets from the Before—"

"The problem," I said, bringing my companions back to reality, "is how we get our hands on any of that. Might I remind you how hard it is to conjure up something from nothing?"

Manufacturing cubes of meat for hungry dragon locks seemed to be about the limit of my abilities in that regard.

"I don't think we can magic a grand piano into existence for her. Though come to think of it, I bet she'd love something noisy like that. Imagine how much she could express herself then."

Bryn looked wistful. "It's a pity. If I had the run of some ruins, I could rustle something up."

"Oh?" I raised an inquiring eyebrow and waited. We still knew very little about Bryn's past. Maybe she felt like talking.

"That's what I spent most of my life doing before I

came here. I was a treasure hunter or a retrieval specialist or a scrap scavenger or whatever you called it in your colony. The easy pickings were long gone, of course, but I never much liked easy anyway."

She grinned. "Easy doesn't give you an excuse to use explosives."

"Explosives?" I shared a concerned look with Ameline. Having a roomie who was a firebug was worrisome enough. I wasn't sure how I felt about the explosives thing.

But it did sound like a cool job.

Bryn either missed our shared glance or chose to ignore it.

"Sure. Huge sections of the city were ruined, and like I said, the easy pickings—anything simple to get to —was already gone. So I would make a nice big explosion to shift some of the rubble, and bam, I'd have a whole new world to explore."

"Did your dad teach you that?" I asked. "Um, when he wasn't drunk, I mean."

Her happy excitement drained away, and I immediately regretted the question.

"The only thing my father taught me was how to dodge him when he was drunk and how to sit around on my ass and carve chunks of wood into prettier chunks of wood. That's what he did for trading when he was sober. But I never liked sitting around. I preferred any activity that got me out of the house."

"Ah." I couldn't help but compare her experience with my own father. Stars, I missed him.

Bryn jammed another log onto the already chock-full fireplace.

"I suppose that's one thing I could do." She sounded reluctant. "If we could get some timber and one or two tools, I could carve something for Millicent."

Ameline was far more enthusiastic. "That's a great idea."

"Or," Bryn said, "I noticed there's a timber section of the external wall where we run laps every morning that's looking damp and prone to start rotting. I could char it with fire to preserve it."

I didn't even need to glance at Ameline this time. No way were we letting Bryn loose on Millicent with a magical flamethrower. We spoke in unison.

"Let's go with the first thing."

Ameline managed to wheedle a mallet, saw, and chisels out of Glenn and Glennys, and we went to bed early. Not to get a full night's sleep. Who had time for that? But so we could wake in the middle of the night to carry out the next step.

When that ungodly hour came, Millicent did not illuminate the wall lamps for us. But Bryn threw more wood on the fire so we didn't waste magic on lighting while we made our preparations.

There was no rain or wind to cover the noises made, so we walked through the hallways with careful steps and kept conversation to a whisper. Ameline's wand lit the way.

We visited the office I'd broken into all those fateful nights ago first. No one had interrogated me or thrown me into a basement dungeon in the days since, so it seemed it my intrusion had gone unnoticed. But if we wanted to win Millicent over, repairing the wardrobe seemed like a necessary step.

Bryn and Ameline stood lookout while I picked the lock, and a moment later we were inside.

Unease trickled through me. Probably because of my horrifying experience with that damn circlet. Few nights passed without my waking in a cold sweat from a nightmarish echo of what I'd felt under its influence.

The same unease didn't affect my companions.

"Cool," Bryn crooned, running her fingers over the nearest trinkets and treasures.

Ameline was staring at the bookshelf on the far wall like she was wondering whether the professor would notice if a few volumes went missing. But she stayed by the door. It didn't matter that no one had forbidden us from exploring the manor. Entering a locked office was almost painful to her rule-abiding nature.

I left them to it and strode to the wardrobe. It opened without resistance. Ignoring my reluctance to lean inside, I pushed aside the hangers of fabric to see the damage.

Except there wasn't any.

My heart sped up. There was no doubt this was the

right room. Which meant someone or something else had repaired that wardrobe.

I was wrong. My intrusion hadn't gone unnoticed. They just hadn't figured out it was me yet.

My gaze flew to the desk. The small iron chest wasn't there.

I backed up. "Let's get out of here. Now," I hissed. "Someone else repaired the cupboard."

Ameline's eyes widened, and I joined her at the door. Bryn caressed a gem-encrusted vase a final time before joining us too. Then we distanced ourselves from the scene of the crime as quickly and quietly as we could.

It didn't take long to reach the large double doors we used to access the manor grounds every morning. Millicent made no attempt to stop us going through them.

The manicured grass and looming forest were even eerier at night. But with the three of us armed with wands and our resolve to stick close to both each other and the sentinel hedge cats, we'd be okay. At least that's what we were counting on.

Bryn had declared all the firewood we had in our room for too dry for carving. So we were here to find a suitable starting piece.

We'd anticipated being outside after dark would be creepy. The moon hung heavy in the sky, illuminating the mist drifting over the grass and the breath exiting our lungs. The night was cold but still, and the stillness meant we could hear every rustling leaf and snapping twig and hair-raising growl or shriek.

We also heard something we didn't anticipate. Voices.

Two kids, the hoods on their cloaks concealing their identities, were standing at the edge of the forest, arguing.

We spotted them before they noticed us, so we crept nearer, using one of the giant hedge cats to cover our approach. We halted when the words became audible.

"They're close. I can feel it."

I knew that voice. Smooth and confident and a little slimy. Jayden, the mayor's kid from Lewiston.

"Then why not wait here until they arrive?"

I recognized the second voice too but didn't know his name. One of Jayden's crew.

He sounded scared.

"Because!" Jayden's tone changed to a vicious hiss. "I don't want to spend one more night in this dung heap. We've already proven we can survive the forest with the help of these wands. Do you really want to test yourself against whatever they cook up for the third trial?"

"Well... no, but—"

"If you don't come with me, I'll tell everyone you're already dead. So they won't bother coming for you. Not ever."

Understanding dawned. Jayden thought his daddy's promised rescue party were nearby and wanted to run off into the forest to meet them.

That took guts. But then if he was oh so confident in

his plan, why was he trying to intimidate this other kid into going with him?

I shared a glance with Bryn and Ameline, and we stepped out into the open.

I'd never had much tolerance for bullying.

"Going somewhere?" I asked.

The two guys jumped like I'd tossed a bucket of ice water over their heads. Their packs thumped against their backs, and Jayden's pale face flushed with anger or embarrassment.

"What's it to you, walker lover?"

I flashed my teeth. "If *you* leave, Jayden, the whole academy will celebrate. But there's no need to drag this poor kid to his death with you."

"I'm not going to die, dumbass. I'm going to be rescued and get the hell out of this place."

Bryn snorted. "Rescued, huh? I suppose you are a bit of a damsel."

Jayden's face got more flushed.

The slender, red-haired kid with him looked from Jayden to us and back again. Then sidled a step closer to us.

In actual fact, I didn't want Jayden to run off into the forest, betting on a rescue party that might never come. But I was hoping if we could prevent his unwilling companion from going with him, Jayden would chicken out. Would see reason and realize his plan was a death sentence.

I softened my tone. "Seriously, guys. The only reason

we survived the first trial in the forest was because we were all together. Even then we might have died without Theus and Lirielle's aid."

It was the wrong tack to take.

"The walkers!" Jayden spat. His fists clenched so hard they shook. "They're the whole problem, not our freaking saviors!"

The other kid sidled another step nearer to us.

I inclined my head. "We know that. But you're still more likely to survive the next few days here at the academy than you are in the forest. Like your friend said, why not wait for the rescue team to arrive?"

Jayden stamped—actually stamped—his foot like a three-year-old. "No!" He lunged forward and grabbed the second guy's cloak. "C'mon, Noah. Let's go."

It was ridiculous, but Jayden was hauling the smaller boy backward, out past the protection of the hedge cats, so I lunged forward too and grabbed his arm.

If the disagreement hadn't been so deadly serious, I would have laughed at this absurd game of tug of war.

Jayden gave up reasoning with us and focused back on Noah. "If you ever want to see your parents again, you better stop dragging your feet and come with me right now."

Poor Noah's face flickered with uncertainty and longing. Jeez, I knew how that felt.

"That's enough," Bryn snapped. Her wand was pointed at Jayden's face. "Let go, or I swear I'll blast a ball of fire straight into your pretty face. Imagine the scarring."

Jayden's *pretty face* twisted into something that wasn't pretty at all. His wand arm came up.

"You know I'll be faster," Bryn said. "I'm good at fire."

Jayden's wand faltered. He let Noah go.

"Fine, stay here, you stinking cowards. I hope you die and have your blood sucked out by the walkers."

He turned and strode into the forest.

We watched him go in silence. I think we all expected him to come back. That it was just a bluff.

But his solitary figure was soon swallowed by shadows the moonlight did not penetrate.

Five long minutes later, he hadn't returned.

Ameline broke our shocked vigil. "Are you okay?" she asked Noah.

"I-I guess. But... what if he's right?"

"He isn't," Ameline said simply. And Noah seemed to take her at her word.

## CHAPTER 19

The next morning, we found Jayden's body—or what was left of it—on the lawn.

In fact, *everyone* found Jayden's body on the front lawn. We were spilling out of the manor for Cricklewood's class when the first girl screamed.

The class was canceled. And some of our classmates threw up for reasons other than too much exercise.

Noah was one of them.

"Is this our fault?" Ameline whispered. "Maybe we should've fetched a professor."

I shook my head—even though my own gut was one giant knot of misery.

"No. Jayden was, for all intents and purposes, an adult."

Not a very mature one, but still. No one sent here to trade their life for their family's should be treated as a child.

"He had the right to make his own decision, and he wouldn't have thanked us for taking it from him."

Ameline looked only mildly reassured.

"Besides," I added, "even if we'd run to the nearest professor, we might've been too late. Or they might not have bothered to do anything. They've made it clear our lives aren't the priority around here."

Ameline's frown deepened like the possibility of uncaring teachers had never occurred to her, but she nodded.

I hugged her. "We saved Noah. Concentrate on that."

Then we went to the dining hall to stare at the breakfast neither of us would eat.

Bryn was already there, shoveling food into her petite frame like a reverse magic trick. I didn't know if that made her strong or uncaring. Or maybe just hungry. She *had* spent hours last night carving the mahogany wood we'd found before she'd finally returned to bed.

I didn't tell her or Ameline my other thoughts about Jayden's death.

The lawn thing bothered me. If a wild animal had killed Jayden, why would it drag its kill onto the manicured lawn that stank of humans and walkers? For that matter, how would it have gotten past the sentinel hedge cats that kept the academy grounds safe?

Was it possible one of the walkers had been responsible? A teacher even? And if so, for what reason?

Maybe it was a warning. To stop anyone else from trying to run. Or maybe I was being paranoid.

I had no proof, nothing remotely concrete, and what it insinuated scared the hell out of me. Which was why I wasn't about to put the idea in my friends' heads unless or until there was something we could do about it.

We needed to learn more. To find answers. More than two weeks had passed, and we were no closer to understanding the walkers' motives. To knowing what was coming after the trial phase. To being able to protect each other and prepare ourselves.

But for any of that to happen, we needed to do more snooping. Which meant our first step hadn't changed. We had to win over Millicent.

But before that, we had to get through another day of classes.

No one had particularly liked Jayden, but his death hit the students—at least the human students—hard all the same. The mood was somber. A few of the faces we passed in the hall were tear-streaked, others unusually pale, and almost no one was joking around. Conversations, when they took place at all, were conducted in whispers.

Yet except for that one canceled class, everything continued as normal, leaving us little time or headspace for grief.

Theus approached me after our Rudimentary Magic lesson. "Are you all right?"

"Why do you ask?"

"Because you smell of the forest. And one of the humans was killed in there mere hours ago."

I tucked away the information that walkers had a sense of smell to rival a dog's, and instead of answering I asked, "What do you know about that?"

He studied me, perhaps trying to work out what was behind my question. Suspicion? Curiosity? Reluctance to answer *his* question?

I wasn't entirely sure myself.

"Very little," he said after a pause. "I don't understand why the boy would leave the safety of the academy grounds when he was not strong enough to defend himself."

*He left to get away from you,* I thought. Not Theus specifically, but walkers in general.

I rummaged around for a more acceptable response. "I'm okay, I guess. Thanks for asking."

"Of course," he said and made to leave.

On a whim, I asked, "Are *you* okay?"

If he was going to pretend to be my friend, it was a fair question. Even though I couldn't imagine a walker being affected by the snuffing out of a human life.

His lips tugged upward in the way I never knew whether to interpret as amusement at the strange human or something more genuine.

"I am. Thank you."

Within a few days, the bulk of the students went back to being too consumed with their own troubles to dwell on Jayden's death. There were rumors flying around that the next trial was imminent. And where before Jayden's body had shown up, every day that had passed without a trial had been greeted with relief, now each passing hour without the next trial being announced only added to the mounting tension.

It was illogical, really. It was not as if Jayden's death had been caused by the academy. Not directly. Yet his sudden and violent demise made our own mortality feel far too real. And our successes in the last two trials were no longer as reassuring.

None of that stopped Bryn working on the gift for Millicent though.

The night she completed it, the three of us snuck out of our room. We might have waited until daylight, but Bryn didn't want the other students knowing she was the artist, and she'd designed it to hang above the manor's front doors.

Millicent did little to impede our passage. I chose to take that as a good sign.

It was strange to be outside after dark again. None of us brought up what happened three nights ago just fifty yards away. We just clustered together on the steps and appraised the manor's entrance.

"How are we going to hang it?" Ameline asked, voice quiet.

*It* was beautiful. An ornate letter *M* carved from rich mahogany timber. Bryn might not like woodcarving much, but she was darn good at it.

"Magic maybe." I didn't like the idea of marring the

piece of art with a nail, and I didn't want Millicent taking offense if we dared to hammer something into her mortar.

"Magic," Bryn agreed.

She was too short to reach the top of the doors. But magic provided a solution to that too. She and I aimed our wands together at the beautifully embellished *M*. We wanted to demonstrate the gift was from both of us, and we also didn't want to send it smashing to the steps because of a momentary distraction.

The *M* floated up without a hitch and neatly adhered itself to the stone surface.

"How'd you make it stick?" I asked her.

"I didn't. I thought you did that?"

The three of us stared at Bryn's handiwork. The carved mahogany timber resting against the pale stone backdrop looked good. Like it had always belonged there.

"I think Millicent must have accepted your gift," Ameline proclaimed in a proud parent sort of way.

There was one way to know for sure.

We rushed on quiet feet to the girls' bathroom.

Bryn, in honor of her hard work, went first.

"Ohhh," she moaned in bliss under the steaming showerhead. "It's hot. And it's freaking marvelous."

I grinned and turned on my own tap. Sure enough, the water that came out was warm. I ran my fingers through it to make sure.

Yes!

My body hummed in delicious anticipation, ready to enjoy my first wondrous experience of a hot shower. A luxury Ameline had been trying not to rave about *too* much for the entire two and a half weeks since we'd arrived out of consideration for my feelings.

Still grinning, I stepped under the spray.

For a fleeting second, I experienced what the others must every time they stepped into one of these stalls.

Then the water turned freezing cold.

My eyes sprang open at the shock of it, and I swear I saw ice chips swirling down the drain.

Damn, damn, and double damn.

Millicent had only forgiven Bryn.

---

I spent the next week lamenting that in all my efforts to prepare for life after the runegate, none of the skills I'd acquired were useful for winning over a snotty, grudge-holding sentient manor.

Funny how I hadn't anticipated the need for that.

I was beginning to wonder if Millicent might enjoy holding a grudge more than any gift I could conjure up.

I mean, I *had* helped with the carving. At least I'd tried. I'd helped find the piece of mahogany timber. I'd gone with Ameline to talk Glenn and Glennys into giving us the tools. And I'd fetched Bryn her meals and read our study notes aloud until my voice went hoarse to buy her time for carving.

I was getting desperate.

Time was speeding by, the season growing colder with the approach of winter. Some mornings the frosted grass crunched under our boots as we ran laps around the lawn.

We were almost a third of the way through the trial phase, and I was no closer to understanding the sinister purpose underlying it all, nor what would happen at the end of it.

How could I protect Ameline, protect anyone, if I didn't know what was coming?

What if excelling at our studies and the trials wasn't enough? What if—despite what Dunraven and Theus had claimed—there weren't supposed to be any human survivors? Because nearly a month after stepping through the runegate, I hadn't seen hide nor hair of a single surviving firstborn from a previous year.

Not to mention Bryn was threatening to go snooping without me unless I thought of something fast. And she'd probably drag Ameline along with her.

I walked down the noisy, creaking stairway, trying to come up with fresh ideas. Maybe I could slay a creature in the next trial, preserve its skin, and stretch it over a pot to make a drum for Millicent to bang. Since she liked expressing herself so much and all.

Unfortunately, I knew how long it took to cure a skin. Maybe I could speed up the process with magic...

I was trying to work out if that was feasible when I literally tripped over a new idea.

The dining hall rug.

Ameline and Bryn had sent me to return the carving tools to the golin as if that might change Millicent's mind about me.

I'd agreed mostly because I was feeling restless, chafing at the delays. Chafing at my ever-increasing list of unanswered questions.

I eyed the frayed edge of the rug I'd just tripped over. Maybe my luck was about to change.

The eclectic pattern in reds and blues would've been glorious once. It stretched across the center of the room, softening the large space and adding an opulent, luxurious feel that matched Millicent's ornate high ceilings and the painstaking care that had been given to every detail.

At least it would have done back in the rug's heyday.

But it was faded now, worn in patches and stained in others. It served little purpose other than to muffle students' footsteps.

I would never be able to create something like this from scratch. But maybe, just maybe, I could restore it to its former glory.

I smiled, suddenly certain this was it. Maybe Millicent had even shifted the rug to trip me and draw my attention to it.

Tools forgotten, I climbed onto one of the dining tables for a better view and studied the carpet's faded hues, imagining how they had once shone bright and bold. Visualizing the pattern as it would appear in those rich, vivid colors without the stains marring their geometry. Pictured the fibers whole and unthinned by time.

Then I aimed my wand.

The magic caught me around the neck and dragged me into darkness.

# CHAPTER 20

I woke in the infirmary, the scents of herbs and chemicals pungent in my nostrils. I was tucked so tightly to the bed that at first I thought I was restrained there.

What had happened?

Memory returned and I flushed, feeling stupid. I'd almost killed myself prettying up that darn rug for Millicent. And for all I knew, she didn't even appreciate it.

Whatever magic affinity I might have, it didn't include fixing things. Could *breaking* things be an affinity?

I struggled free of the constricting sheets and sat up. My head swam. My mouth felt like I'd been chewing on Glenn's furry face. And I wanted nothing more than to press my finger against Millicent's wallpaper and see how hard she bit me.

I wondered if they had a mental health wing of the infirmary.

Given the way the room was wobbling, I stayed where I was.

Slowly my vision stabilized, bringing my surroundings into focus. A giant tree dominated the circular space, its trunk a pale silver, its branches stretching to occupy every inch available beneath the glass ceiling. Dozens of narrow hospital-style beds claimed the space below. Not just the floor space either. The beds hung in the air, suspended on silver thread from the branches above.

No wonder whoever was in charge here tucked their patients in so tight.

My own bed was on the second level of floating mattresses. High enough that an uncontrolled landing would hurt but not so high that I couldn't climb down.

Well, under normal circumstances anyway. Right now my body wasn't offering me peak performance.

The room was quiet. Almost eerily so. I could see only one other bed that was occupied.

"Hello?" I called.

No answer.

I heaved out a sigh. How long would they expect me to stay here lying quietly? I had things to do, buildings to befriend, and more homework than you could wave a wand at.

My next thought was disconcerting. How long had I already been here? An hour? A day? More?

I glanced at the sole other patient three beds across

on the just-above-the-floor level. *He* looked like he'd been here for ages.

A reddish-brown beard adorned his face, too straggly to be intentional, and yet the length suggested at least two months of growth. His hair too was overlong. But beneath the untidy jumble of beard and hair, he looked young.

My age. And human given the imperfection of his facial hair.

Except I didn't recognize him.

The academy was large enough that I didn't know everyone's names, but their faces were all familiar. His wasn't one of them.

So who the heck was he? And why was he here?

Curiosity overcame the wisdom of resting any longer. I shed the last of the covers, swung my legs over the side of the bed, and tried for a controlled descent.

What I *got* was a crash-landing with the blankets tumbling down around my head.

Newly grateful that no one else was here—no one awake that is—I wrested myself free of the bedding a final time and made my way over to the mystery man.

"Hey," I said.

He didn't respond.

I "accidentally" bumped the bed. "Are you awake?"

Nothing.

I shook his arm gently. It was warm at least, but he didn't stir a whit.

Feeling faintly irritated (okay, so I get cranky when I'm sick), I poked him in the ribs. Hard.

Nothing.

Which was about the time I came to realize he was probably not just asleep.

Drugged then, or unconscious. Maybe even comatose.

He was thin, and the circles under his eyes were so dark they appeared bruised. But there were no physical injuries that I could see. Pulling back the blanket to check felt like a step too far even for me.

"Oh, Nova, you're awake."

I whirled in the direction of the speaker to see a walker woman entering the room. She was dark and willowy with a kind but stern face and clear gray eyes.

"I'm Healer Invermoore, and I expected you to be out longer yet."

She smiled as she said it. Like it was a pleasant surprise rather than an inconvenience. "How are you feeling?"

"I'm fine," I told her, more because I wanted to return to my friends than because it was true.

A trace of amusement suggested she saw right through my deception. But she was unruffled by it.

"That *is* good news."

Something about her was more approachable than the other walkers. Something that made me try my luck by waving my hand at the unconscious guy in the bed and asking, "Who is he? I don't recognize him."

"A student from a previous year."

Shock and my lingering weakness made me grab the bed rail for support.

The sole firstborn that anyone's seen from another year, and he's comatose?

"What happened?" I asked. "Did he fail one of the trials?"

Healer Invermoore's expression remained serene. "No, he passed them all. He was one of the few selected to continue."

My gut tightened. The still figure in the bed was one of the *successful* kids?

"Then what happened?" I asked again.

Theus had told me most of the kids from previous years were still alive. Had he lied? Except the guy behind me was *technically* alive. And I remembered Theus modifying his answer with a muttered "sort of."

Is this what he'd meant?

The healer stepped up to the bed and looked down at the guy in question. The patient she must've cared for, tending to all his bodily needs, for months. Maybe years.

She straightened the blankets around his motionless form—the ones I'd mussed in my ill-considered attempts to wake him.

If I wasn't so afraid of what his comatose state might signify, I would've been feeling rather embarrassed about that now.

The silence stretched too long. Long enough that I thought she wasn't going to answer.

But at last she said, "Those who are selected to continue with the academy undergo a kind of transformation ritual. He came out of his like this."

She finished adjusting the blankets.

"But he may yet wake up. One day."

She shifted her gaze to me then and must have caught something in my expression that made her realize she'd said too much. Shock. Horror. Confusion. I didn't know what my face showed. But hers shut down as a result.

She wasn't going to say another word. Not on the topic of the comatose kid.

But she did have plenty to say about taking care of myself.

I barely heard a word of it. Over the past month, the majority of my focus had been on surviving and passing the training and trial period. And of doing everything I could to make sure Ameline passed the trial period with me.

Sure, I'd wanted to know what was coming afterward, wanted to gather information so I could devise my own plans. But I'd always assumed we'd figure it out eventually.

Now—for the first time since Dunraven had given us his little introductory lecture—I wondered if knowing would not be enough to save us.

# CHAPTER 21

Millicent forgave me.

But my joy over that accomplishment was tempered by the news we had a trial tonight.

And the haunting image of the boy in the bed. Utterly unresponsive.

I suppose his fate was better than Jayden's. But Jayden had been a coward, a bully, and a fool. Spoiled by his father and unprepared for life at the academy.

All this time I'd been thinking that if I could just be good enough, perform well enough, prepare hard enough, and bide my time long enough, I might have a chance at bringing down this whole institution.

But the comatose kid, he'd *been* good enough. He'd been selected. And now he was stuck in that bed, unable to open his eyes, let alone fulfill his heart's secret desires.

Between Jayden and me, maybe I was the bigger fool.

But I didn't have time to dwell on that now, because I had a trial to get to.

Healer Invermoore had recommended I stay in the infirmary and sit this one out. I'd come close to killing myself fixing that rug, blowing through every bit of power I had and most of my physical life force besides. She said the closer you came to flaming out, the longer those stores took to replenish. So I needed to be extra cautious about expending too much magic.

But Ameline and I had promised each other that we were in this together, and I wasn't about to let her risk her life alone. So I joined my roommates and the rest of the students assembled on the lawn.

Unfortunately, my good intentions didn't count for much.

All the professors were there, but it was Grimwort who stood before the tables piled high with a large assortment of peculiar equipment. He graced us with a pinched look that suggested patience was a virtue he hadn't mastered and announced, "Each student will be facing the next trial alone."

Dammit.

Was it too late to slink back to the infirmary?

I exchanged glances with my companions. A worried one with Ameline. A raised eyebrow with Bryn.

"Oh, that reminds me…" Bryn detached a wrapped dagger from her belt and offered it to me. "I know you lost yours in the first trial. I've been using my new Millicent privileges to acquire a few things."

I thought *acquired* might mean *pinched*, but it didn't stop me from sliding the weapon through my pocket into the sheath on my thigh.

I'd missed my old dagger, but there always seemed to be more pressing matters than working out how to replace it. Except somehow Bryn had found time to do it for me.

My throat tightened at the gesture. "Thank you."

The blade's weight was especially welcome now. I would be facing this new trial with very limited magic.

My attention returned to the front and found Grimwort's cold gaze aimed our way.

Oops.

He resumed his bored droning. "This challenge will test your wits and your ability to conserve your magic. So use your meager supplies of both wisely."

I grimaced. As opposed to nearly killing yourself prettying up a rug, I supposed he meant.

"The difficulty of the trial will be adjusted according to your magical capacity. By now you should each have identified where your affinity lies. I suggest you make use of that knowledge."

His suggestion made sense. Casting spells within your affinity meant more powerful magic with less drain.

The problem was, I still hadn't figured out my affinity.

Everyone else's had been obvious after the first week of Rudimentary Magic lessons. People tended to instinctively use tiny amounts of magic in their everyday lives without realizing it. Ameline's affinity was with animals. Bryn's was with heat, flames, and explosions—no surprises there. And mine?

Well, it definitely *wasn't* with the restoration of old rugs. Beyond that, I had no clue.

My saving grace to date was that I had more magic than most. But that wasn't going to help me now when the difficulty was adjusted accordingly.

I was really starting to regret getting out of that nice, comfy infirmary bed.

Even if it had been hanging from a tree.

"You may now come forward and select one item from the tables to aid you in your challenge."

"What will we be facing in the trial?" someone asked.

Grimwort showed his teeth in something that wasn't a smile. "You'll find out once you've chosen your item."

Bryn rolled her eyes. "Typical."

But she looked more excited than exasperated. She was an odd duck.

Grimwort raised his voice over the chatter as everyone pushed toward the tables.

"After you've chosen your item, see one of the professors, who will translocate you to your individual test. The trial begins as soon as you arrive."

After the speech Grimwort just gave, most students were choosing an object that aligned with their affinity. Bryn picked up some kind of explosive powder, Ameline chose a sack of grain—animal feed presumably—and a kid who had a knack with plants selected a packet of seeds.

But I didn't have that option. I mulled over the items, trying to think. To logic my way through the dilemma.

Without an affinity for it, a sackful of grain wasn't going to do me much good, and the same rationale ruled out a bunch of the other items. I wandered back to the weapons tables again.

The last two trials had mostly been about fighting and defending ourselves. And recent history revealed walkers were a violent lot. Not to mention Grimwort was a jerk who made it clear he believed teaching humans magic was a waste of time. He wouldn't care if there were a few less kids to teach.

My hand hovered over the bow and its quiver of arrows. I had the dagger Bryn had given me. Whether or not Grimwort *knew* I had it was beside the point. So should I opt for a long-range weapon to complement it?

I'd learned to use bows and Before-style guns and was a decent shot with both, but I was better with a dagger. Bullets could only be used once, and arrows broke, or fletching got damaged when you trained. Whereas a dagger could be used over and over again and only needed to be sharpened afterward.

The weapon I was considering was a shortbow, but it would still be unwieldy if I had to run or scramble through the tangled forest undergrowth with a monster on my heels. I wasn't cocky enough to think myself above fleeing.

That and the fact bows needed both forewarning and distance to draw made me leave it on the table.

Grimwort had been talking about *magical* affinities, but I would follow his advice in the physical sense.

I was best with a dagger.

They were useful at short and medium range, weren't unwieldy, and could be used indefinitely. So long as you didn't lose them anyway.

The daggers were of just as fine make as the bow. I picked up an unadorned one—made for utility rather than decoration—and tested the balance of it appreciatively. It came with its own belt sheath, so I strapped it beside my wand.

Half the students had already disappeared, waved through gateways by one professor or another, I rejoined Bryn and Ameline where they were hanging back at the end of an informal queue, waiting for me.

This was it then. We'd each be facing whatever lay on the other side of those gateways alone.

I forced a note of cheery confidence into my voice.

"Good luck."

The words were so feeble, so inadequate. But I couldn't bring myself to even consider the possibility that one of us might not come back.

"And try not to wear yourselves out. We've got snooping to do tonight now that Millicent no longer wants to bury me beneath her basement."

Bryn snapped a mock salute. "Yes, ma'am."

Ameline choked on something that was half laugh, half sob.

I hugged her and spoke into her ear. "I love you. No matter what happens, we're still in this together, okay?"

She nodded against my shoulder. "Right back at you."

We turned as one and hugged Bryn too.

"Eww, get off me, you pervs," she protested. But she hugged us back, and I thought she might've swiped at one of her eyes afterward.

Then we were at the front of the line and the teachers were waving us forward. Ameline went to Professor Fenfurrell, our botany teacher. Bryn to Cricklewood.

I went to Dunraven. "Your only objective is to reach the ground alive," he told me quietly. "Speed is less important than magic conservation and wits."

Still processing the words, I stepped through my personal gateway. And almost went plummeting to my death.

# CHAPTER 22

I was standing on a small, circular platform about three feet in diameter. Beyond that, there was nothing but air.

Low-hanging clouds—at least I hoped they were low-hanging—floated around me, smearing my vision. But in the distance I could see dozens and dozens of ivory-colored columns stretching into the sky.

Many were shorter than mine, and I could just make out kids standing or crouching on top like I was. Some farther away extended far past my own.

All of them were too tall to fall from with any hope of surviving.

Guess that's what our magic was for.

I should have chosen the rope.

I sank into a crouch to lower my center of gravity and leaned over the edge to gauge the distance.

The dizzying height made me curse. Then curse again. I was about three hundred feet up.

I supposed I should be grateful that I'd spent too many years jogging up and down skyscraper stairwells to be afraid of heights.

Still, I'd have to be a fool not to fear this one. There were no safety rails. No Before-style rock climbing harnesses. And no way down except one I might conjure for myself.

I huddled into my cloak to ward off the chill and tried to think. Even if I *had* selected the rope, there wasn't anything to secure it to. Were the items we'd picked a distraction? Or were they just making sure the trial wasn't too easy if you were lucky enough to pick a *useful* object?

I kept my senses alert to my surroundings in case of attack, but I had a sinking suspicion that this test wasn't about fighting. Which meant the dagger was about the worst object I could've chosen.

Forget my weapons then. I'd figure something else out.

I considered my options. My minimal magic options.

Even if I hadn't flamed out so recently, there was no way I had enough power to fly or float down. Grimwort had made us practice summoning a small amount of wind to blow our books off the desk, then catch them as they fell. It had been challenging and exhausting.

Moving objects with telekinesis was easier than mastering the wind, but I hadn't moved anything half as heavy as myself. If moving oneself was even possible. I didn't have magic to spare for experimenting now, and if it worked, I wasn't about to trust my life to being able to maintain it all the way down.

It was a very, very long way down.

Could I shrink the pillar itself? Compress it somehow? Or sink it into the earth maybe? I peered over the edge again and discarded the plan. The column might only be three feet wide, but it was incredibly tall. And that made for a *lot* of volume to morph or bury. Too much.

Growing a plant to spring up from the earth and save me was equally unfeasible. I knew from my botany classes that I had about as much knack for growing things as an egg has for flying.

So what else did I have on hand?

My daggers might be useless, but perhaps my leather belt that held the newest one at my hip would help. I could lengthen it with magic, and it would hold my weight. But extending a piece of leather to hundreds of times its original size was beyond me.

I chewed my lip.

I'd heard about how people used to climb trees with the aid of a rope or strap. They'd loop it around the trunk and their own bodies, then use it for leverage to work their way up and down. But the technique relied on the tree's textured bark for grip—to stop their feet and the strap from slipping.

The platform beneath me looked smooth. Too smooth.

In case appearances were deceiving, I ran my hands over the surface. The material was unfamiliar. It had the appearance of stone but felt almost warm beneath my fingers. And though it was hard, not giving at all beneath my weight, it felt less solid, less dense than stone might. Like it was porous and would weigh less than stone. Maybe less than timber.

It was, however, as smooth as it looked.

Ugh.

Frustrated and acutely aware of time passing, I stabbed the stupid pillar with my useless dagger. The tip of the blade slid in with little resistance. Like a fork into an uncooked potato. Pulling it out required equal if not more force.

Interesting.

I stabbed the pillar a bunch more times, testing different sections, angles, and weight-bearing capacities. The weird properties of whatever material it was might just offer me a way down.

A non-magical way down.

Well, they wanted us to conserve our magic, didn't they?

It was the best idea I'd had.

That didn't mean it was good.

But hey, if it didn't work, I had such a long way to fall that I might come up with a better one on the way down.

I drove my two daggers deep into the side of the pillar and prepared myself to descend. I magically stretched and strengthened my leather belt. I secured my cloak so it wouldn't get in the way. And I put my wand between my teeth, trying *very* hard not to think about what it was made from. No creatures had attacked me from the sky yet, but both my hands were going to be occupied, and I didn't want to be left defenseless.

Then I lowered myself over the edge.

To my intense relief, the blades stayed lodged in the pillar as I hung the full weight of my body from the dagger's handles.

I swallowed. Maybe for the last time. *Here goes nothing.*

I yanked one of the daggers out and slammed it in again two feet below the first. Then, painstakingly switching arms and blades to hang from, I repeated the process with the dagger on the left.

Damn. This was going to hurt.

I was strong and fit, but the mechanics involved put intense strain on my arms. And I found a new appreciation for all the strength exercises Cricklewood made us do.

Thirty feet down the pillar, I decided this was a *terrible* idea.

Every two feet I descended sent lances of pain spiking down my shoulders and back. My limbs were trembling, and I was so far off halfway that it might be smarter attempting to climb back up than continuing down.

I needed to think about something other than the

pain. The mind was powerful. And when the need was great enough, the body could dig deep and accomplish feats that seemed impossible.

So I thought about how my friends were doing. Imagined meeting them at the bottom. Ameline's face lighting up when she saw me safe. Bryn smugly pointing out how she'd saved my ass with that dagger.

Each thrust of my blades into the strange, porous surface reminded me of that first day with Millicent.

If these columns turned out to be sentient, I didn't want to even *begin* to imagine what I'd have to do to earn a pardon.

I'd made it another thirty feet.

But despite the cold air and the colder wind, I was starting to sweat. Not a good combination when my grip on the daggers was the only thing between me and death.

It wasn't long after that before my sweat-dampened fingers turned numb from the cold.

Numb, slippery, and fatigued. What could possibly go wrong?

I'd made it another thirty feet and was now about a third of the way down.

I needed to rest.

This was what I'd lengthened my belt for. I'd envisaged hooking it over the two dagger hilts and then looping it under my butt as a sort of swing seat, leaning my back against the warm pillar and resting my arms.

But I hadn't envisaged having to orchestrate all that

with wet, frozen fingers and tortured muscles that burned with the fire of a thousand suns. Or maybe just one of Bryn's blazing fires, but still.

I yanked out the topmost dagger. I needed them side by side, about a foot apart, for my swing seat thing to work. But as I prepared to drive it into position, my hand spasmed around the hilt.

The blade fell from my deadened fingers.

Instinct made me lunge to catch it, but I pulled up short before I followed its tumbling descent.

Instead, shaking with exhaustion and adrenaline and dawning horror, I wrapped both hands around the hilt of my remaining dagger.

I was barely a third of the way down. And completely stuck.

Only magic could save me now.

Magic… or a nice quick plummet to my death.

I let go.

# CHAPTER 23

I used both feet to shove myself away from the pillar and toward my target.

Wind roared around me, my cheeks, my hair, as if it were trying to push me upward. But it was only the result of how fast I was falling.

I had to slow myself down.

Focusing was near impossible, but I'd done half of what I needed while I'd still been hanging from the pillar. Awkwardly using my wand to affix my cloak to my wrists and ankles, and detach it from my neck.

Now I rolled until I was doing the world's largest belly-flop and spread-eagled my arms and legs.

My cloak streamed behind me, flapping and twisting to catch the least air possible. The exact opposite of what I wanted. I twisted my neck to aim the wand, still clenched between my teeth, at the thrashing fabric. And visualized it stiffening and smoothing out, like a rectangular, body-sized umbrella. Or an upside-down magic carpet.

I felt when it worked. My rapid descent slowed. Not enough, but some. And the noise of snapping fabric ceased, leaving just the roar of the wind.

My eyes were squinted and tearing against the air's assault, but I scanned the forest below. The forest I was fast approaching. There. A large fenbrosia tree, the kind I knew to have slender but densely packed branches that might help break my fall without breaking my body simultaneously.

Maybe.

I had about two seconds.

One.

I rolled so my stiffened cloak hit first. Branches smashed, bashed, scratched, and walloped me. I protected my head and prayed I'd survive. That I wouldn't be paralyzed or skewered. But I could feel myself slowing down. The tree's beatings coming a little farther apart. Then I slammed into something and stopped.

It was so quiet.

I drew a cautious breath, taking stock. Everything hurt. My head, my back, my front, and every single limb. I supposed I should be grateful they were still attached. My skin was on fire. Actually, there were prob-ably more scratches than skin now. And when I breathed, pain shot through my abdomen.

Okay, a couple of broken or fractured ribs then. But if that was the worst of it, I'd gotten off lightly.

Then again, maybe shock was keeping the worst of the pain at bay.

I opened my eyes. My vision worked, and all my organs were still on the inside. Another excellent result.

Then I looked beyond my poor, broken body and realized I hadn't made it to the ground yet.

I was still seven feet up, caught in the lower branches of the tree. And the thought of using my abused hand, arm, and back muscles to climb down made me want to cry.

Screw it. Perhaps it was the shock or the concussion, but I sat up, rib cage screaming, head spinning, and arms hanging dead at my sides, and let myself fall the final seven feet to the earth.

The jolt of the impact made everything worse. A lot worse. But I had to get to Ameline. To Bryn. Had to know they were okay. So I forced myself to stand up. Take one step. Then another.

Dunraven rescued me from torturing myself further. He popped his head through a newly formed gateway and beckoned me back to the lawn.

Ameline and Bryn rushed toward me as soon as my feet touched the grass. I was so relieved to see them both alive that my knees gave way.

They caught me. One on each arm. And I realized they were better than just alive. They looked whole and unharmed. Maybe even perky.

"How'd you get down so fast?" I asked.

Bryn smirked. "With an explosion, what else?"

I raised an eyebrow in question.

Even that hurt.

"I used the explosive powder plus a spark of magic to blow out the base of my pillar, then clung on and magically cushioned myself while it teetered and crashed into a neighboring column. A bit of fire melted and stuck the two together, and then I rode that baby down like a slippery slide. It was so much fun I wanted to do it again."

Her tower couldn't have been half as tall as mine for that to work, but it was a gutsy solution.

Ameline smiled and shook her head. "My technique wasn't quite so—"

"Dramatic? Sensational? Electrifying? Spectacular?" Bryn supplied.

"—I was going to say destructive."

Bryn smirked again. "That too."

"I saw a griffin flying overhead and lured it down with the sack of grain. They're omnivores, you know. Then I used my magic affinity to suggest that if it flew me down to the ground, I would get it some more."

As simple as that.

"Wow. Well played. Both of you."

I was impressed and a tad embarrassed I'd dragged myself out here to protect Ameline and then been so thoroughly trounced.

Bryn eyeballed me. "How did *you* get down?"

"I think I'd better go see Healer Invermoore," I said.

It was true, but more than that, I wanted to postpone the humiliation. So being careful not to breathe deeply nor move my arms (or eyebrows for that matter), I limped my way back to the infirmary bed I never should have vacated.

# CHAPTER 24

Needless to say, we did not go snooping that night. Or the next.

Healer Invermoore managed to knit up my ribs, fix my concussion, and soothe my tortured muscles, but she was limited by my body's meager reserves. She could use magic to greatly speed natural processes, but she couldn't do any more than a patient's life force could provide energy for.

I was healed enough to hold a pen, but that was the extent of my physical activities for a few days. Magically aided healing required rest. Flaming out required rest. And falling hundreds of feet into a tree required rest.

I was even excused from Cricklewood's classes, though he made me sit in the rain and watch.

We never had progressed to weapons training. I didn't know if Cricklewood had been messing with us on the first day, or he still thought we were too pathetic to hold a blade. I supposed by walker standards, even our new levels of strength and fitness didn't amount to much.

Millicent's forgiveness was the only silver lining of the whole ordeal. I was looking forward to snooping and finally getting some answers to my many, many questions. But more immediately, I spent every moment I could in the bathroom, soaking under an unending stream of hot water.

My skin wrinkled to the point where if I'd cut the beard off Cricklewood's face and glued it to my own, I could've passed for the old coot.

When I finally recovered, we set about to snooping with a vengeance.

Over the next few weeks—whenever classes and fighting for our lives in the trials hadn't left us too exhausted—we explored every room in the manor. From the ancient wine cellar in the basement to the hidden crawlspaces in the attic and everything in between. Everything, that is, except for the blood-locked dormitories and the few rooms we couldn't find a way into.

But we turned up very little.

There was a small arsenal of medieval weapons locked up on the second floor—which was useful since, despite owning the same dagger for ten years growing up, I seemed to keep misplacing them here. There was a large territorial plant in the attic. And in the professors' shared wing, there were piles of books in different languages and many objects we couldn't fathom the purpose of.

But all in all, the manor appeared to be what the walkers claimed. A training ground for students housed in a repurposed and now-sentient manor from the Before. There was a bunch of antique furniture shoved into storage rooms, a few cloth-covered painted portraits of a family who probably lived here before the stairs began to creak, and a salt-damp problem in the basement.

We magicked up the salt damp for Millicent over several nights, careful not to overtax ourselves, and she in turn allowed us free rein. Occasionally she would even warn us when someone was coming.

We'd marked Dunraven's map as we went, and there were very few rooms we hadn't found a way into. But I supposed that if there were places the walkers didn't want us to find, he probably wouldn't include them on the floor plan.

It was only when we'd exhausted our own avenues of investigation that we thought to ask Millicent for help.

"Millicent, do you know what the real purpose of this academy is? Why did the walkers bring us here?"

Ameline spotted it first. A flying lizard with feathers like some long-extinct dinosaur was flapping its wings on the wallpaper. As soon as it had our attention, it began to fly. Through the wallpaper, that is. Other creatures ducked and leaped out of the way. Some waved their paws or puffed up fur or feathers in protest. But the lizard-bird flew on undeterred.

We followed it.

None of us were really surprised when our guide led us down to the basement. That's where all the creepy things are. There was no wallpaper down here, and the lizard-bird was flying across the rough-hewn stones of the manor's footings. It drew us to a corner we'd poked around in before. Not far from the salt-damp problem we'd cleared up.

Then it stopped, perching on one of the stones and ruffling its feathers as if to say *Here, this is what you asked for.*

Except there was nothing there.

Ameline, Bryn, and I glanced at each other, unsure what to try next.

Then an entire section of the wall sank into the floor in near-perfect silence.

Bryn sent a sphere of fiery light into the opening where the wall had just been.

What that light illuminated made my blood run cold.

There was a hospital bed in the middle of the room, one that was similar in style to those in the infirmary. But there the similarities ended.

Where there had been daylight and airy openness, there was darkness and unbroken stone walls. Where there had been a feeling of nurture and well-being, there was an ambience both sinister and disturbing.

The walls were unadorned rough-hewn rock. The floor was the bare earth. And spread around the bed was some kind of arcane circle of creepy objects.

Thick black candles offered the only source of potential light. Various bones, including several human-looking skulls, were carved with hundreds or thousands of tiny runes. Blood-red feathers that appeared too perfect to have come from nature rested upon the soil without any signs of dust. And then there was a locked iron chest. Much like the one that had held the evil circlet I still had the occasional nightmare about.

I was leaving *this* chest firmly closed. Whatever nasties were shut away in there could stay locked up.

I backed away a step.

"Basilisk's balls," Bryn breathed beside me.

Somehow I'd completely forgotten she was there. Too transfixed by the creepy room to remember softer, happier things like friends and light and life.

I leaped half a foot in the air like a sprayed cat. And then felt a surge of gratitude for her and Ameline's companionship.

The lizard-bird guide was still here too—waiting on the section of wall that hadn't sunk into the earth.

Why had Millicent brought us here?

To scare us?

To warn us?

To keep her company over the long nights by ensuring we might never sleep again?

But I remembered the question we'd asked her: *Why*

*did the walkers bring us here?* And thought again of the comatose boy in the infirmary. Of Healer Invermoore's words to me. That the successful students would go through a transformation ritual and that he'd come out of his like that. With so little left that he hadn't moved since.

And I had a horrible feeling that this was where that "transformation ritual" took place...

# CHAPTER 25

Millicent showed me one more thing about a week later. Just me this time.

She nudged me gently from sleep (I was so glad we'd gotten past the flinging-me-onto-the-floor thing), and when I saw she hadn't woken Bryn or Ameline, I decided to trust her choice.

Even if the others would kill me when they found out.

The lizard-bird guide was back. It led me down to the first floor, near one of the old servant entrances that were usually kept locked, and guided me into a small room that might've once been a walk-in pantry.

I stood quietly in the blackness, waiting to learn why Millicent had brought me here. Then I heard something. The faintest scuff of a shoe over floorboards. And a pinprick of light appeared at eye level before me.

A peephole.

Not even breathing, I pressed my eye against the new aperture.

Then *he* stepped into view.

My stomach dropped all the way to my ankles.

Fletcher.

I hadn't seen him in two years, but I knew him instantly. Every part of me screamed in recognition.

And yet...

Though his face was exactly the way I had remembered—except for a small scar above his right eye and his black hair longer than he used to keep it—some instinct warned me he was not the man I once knew.

It wasn't the new muscles, or the strange clothes and weapons, or the extra inch of height.

It was the way he moved. Like he was walking from one nightmare into another.

It was the lack of expression on his achingly familiar face. The one I'd loved to watch because it so rarely stayed still for more than a moment.

It was the lack of light or warmth in his dark brown eyes. The bleak dullness that had replaced it.

My chest felt tight and my own eyes burned.

What had they done to him?

If the order of his birth hadn't ripped all choice from him, Fletcher would've been a teacher. The man I remembered was gentle and kind and good, with a smile that brightened any room he was in. And that smile would always include everyone.

He might not have been conventionally attractive,

but affection colored him handsome. Fletcher never left anyone out. His unfailing warmth extended to everybody, and kids used to follow him around to bask in his presence.

Next to him, I'd always felt that everything would be okay. No matter what else was going on. No matter what our futures held.

But *this* Fletcher? *This* version of my friend?

I dug my fingernails into my palms, throat too constricted to swallow.

A large part of me—the part that had grown up with Fletcher's teasing and laughter and support—wanted to shove open the door and run to him, but I didn't move.

The man in front of me wasn't *my* Fletcher. I didn't know who he was. Not anymore.

Besides, Millicent had hidden me here for a reason, and I didn't want to betray her trust.

So I stood frozen in place, eyes burning but dry, and watched him knock on the door at the end of the corridor.

Cricklewood opened it and ushered Fletcher inside. The door shut me out of their conversation but not before I heard Cricklewood order, "Report."

Had I been left to my own devices, I might've stood there for as long as it took to catch one more glimpse. But my lizard-bird guide urged me back to my dorm room, and I complied on wooden legs.

Minutes later, I crawled into the soft comfort of my bed. Sleep would be a longer time coming.

From day one, the goal had been for Ameline, Bryn, and me to excel at anything the professors threw at us. To distinguish ourselves and make the cut. And except when not knowing my affinity had led to a near-disastrous third trial, I was pretty sure our results had been above average in both trials and classwork.

But seeing Fletcher tonight and the creepy transformation room last week made me second-guess everything.

Now I didn't know what was worse. To succeed and continue with the academy—which meant undergoing the transformation ritual that had put one guy in a coma and destroyed everything I'd loved about my childhood friend.

Or to fail and face a future that was even more unknown.

# CHAPTER 26

More weeks passed, classes continued, and the shock of seeing Fletcher gradually faded in my memory. Perhaps I'd overreacted. The hallway had been dim and shadowy, and we hadn't actually spoken. Maybe my fears had colored the way I'd perceived him.

Even if that wasn't the case, our lives were on the line every time we faced a new trial. The walkers had made it clear they valued results over any risk of death. So if our choices were between winning or failing—winning seemed better for our health.

So we stuck with the plan. We stuck together. And we hoped it would be enough.

Theus had been right. The trials only got harder. But we were growing more competent along with them.

The three of us were shoveling down dinner on yet another Wednesday night when it happened.

The beginning of the end.

All the professors, who usually dined by themselves in a smaller, more elegantly appointed room on the other side of the manor, strode into the dining hall. The walkers moved like a lethal pack of wolves. Wilverness clopping along in her centaur form didn't quite fit in.

There was no need for them to call for our attention. The hum of conversation sputtered and died of its own accord.

Our months at the Firstborn Academy had taught us to fear surprises.

Dunraven stepped forward. "For many of the human students, this will be your last meal at Millicent Manor."

There was a collective intake of breath, and one poor kid started choking on their food. Shocked murmurs rippled around the room. The human side of the room anyway. The walker students had known this was coming.

"In two hours, you will undertake the final trial. Your performance in which will determine your future. Come dawn tomorrow, two lists will be posted in the dining hall. The students on one of those lists will continue with the academy. The students on the second will depart immediately."

I was abruptly regretting eating so fast. Or eating at all. My food sat in my stomach like a wet brick that was trying to work its way back up my throat.

How had this snuck up on us? It must have been three months since the day we'd first stepped through that runegate and given Millicent an excuse to torture Bryn and me for the next couple of weeks. But in everything that had happened to us since—the homesickness and fear, the danger and deaths, the magic and monsters, and the revelations and friendships—time had blurred, and somewhere along the way I'd stopped keeping track.

Three months ago we'd just wanted the training and trials to be over. Now it felt too soon. Too sudden.

My breathing glitched. What if our names were on separate lists?

Ameline must've been thinking the same thing, because she reached out and grabbed my hand hard enough to hurt.

How many times had we made the promise to each other?

*We'll stick together, no matter what. They might take everything else, but they can't take that from us.*

I squeezed her hand back, wishing I could still believe that. Still believe that we had the power to keep that solemn vow.

Bryn noticed our gripped hands, and as brave and independent as she was, I grabbed hers too.

Her composed expression didn't waver, but she gripped just as hard as Ameline did.

This was it then.

---

We stepped through the gateway from the floodlit lawn into the dark forest.

The trial that would determine our fates was similar to the first.

Only this time, instead of dozens of kids pooling their magic and skills, there was just the three of us.

This time the walkers were sitting on the sidelines. An anomaly that made me wonder whether any of us were intended to survive.

And this time, instead of clearing our path of apex predators as the professors had apparently done the first time, they'd be ensuring our paths crossed.

Oh, and it was nighttime. Bringing out a whole bevy of less familiar monsters who could see, smell, and hear better than we could.

In this trial, we would not be assessed on speed and survival alone. No, we'd been trained in strategy, endurance, knowledge of creatures and plants, magic use, and strength of mind and body—and that was what we would be judged by.

Every student was being watched. Every team monitored to ensure they'd be *appropriately challenged.*

In other words, we were like chess pieces in the walkers' game, and they would throw everything at us just to see how we'd react. To decide who was worthy to continue at their little academy.

Our reactions, our performance, would determine not just whether we lived through the night but our entire futures. And worse, whether we would face those futures together—or the walkers would separate us.

They had ripped me away from my home, my life, and my family. I was not sure I could survive them snatching the only precious things I had left. Ameline. And now Bryn too.

Not with my heart intact anyway.

They stood beside me now. The walkers had allowed us this one small mercy at least. As part of testing our ability to strategize, they'd let us choose our small teams for the final trial.

The forest was eerie at night. The verdant beauty that drew me to it during the day was absent, cloaked in shadows. Leaving only the promise of danger.

Jayden had been the first but not the last of our classmates whose lives had been snuffed out by its perils.

The darkness was so thick I could feel it infiltrating my lungs with every breath I took. Making the next harder to draw.

Or maybe that was fear.

But we'd all learned to master our fear in the past three months. The few that hadn't had died in their trials —or wound up in the infirmary with an illness of the mind rather than the body that Invermoore couldn't heal.

So I continued breathing in that darkness, senses alert for attack, until my eyes adjusted.

Thank heavens the sky was clear and the moon was

shining. Not that much of its light trickled through the canopy.

But we couldn't afford to create our own light. It would only draw the monsters to us. So once I could make out as much of our surroundings as I was going to, I shifted my focus to practical matters.

"All right," I murmured with a confidence I didn't feel. "Let's avoid as many of the nasties as we can tonight. To spot them before they spot us, we'll need to use our second sight."

Second sight was one of the more advanced magic techniques we'd been taught by Grimwort. It gave us an alternate way of viewing the world, a kind of secondary vision that overlaid our physical sight and varied from person to person.

Bryn could see the heat signatures of both living and nonliving things. Ameline could locate and identify mind signatures of living beings. And I could see life force energy. Kind of.

None of our magical perceptions were infallible. Bryn's heat vision was unable to see through solid masses. Ameline was blind to minds so different from her own that they were incompatible with her communication magic. And both of them had to be looking in the right direction to see anything coming.

I could sense life force energy in a 360-degree circle around me, but indistinctly, like candlelight flickering behind closed eyelids. It was so faint I needed my eyes shut to perceive it, and for some reason no one would explain, I couldn't see walker students at all.

Still, the combination of our second sights was a heck of a lot better than our naked eyes in this dark forest.

"Let's not do *too* good a job at avoiding the monsters," Bryn countered. "The walkers want a show, so we'll give them one."

"You just want an excuse to burn things."

Her teeth flashed in the gloom, unrepentant. "That too."

Still, she aimed her wand at her head to enable her second sight, and Ameline did the same.

Knowing they were temporarily distracted, I skimmed our shadowy surroundings again.

We were in a small clearing enclosed by trees and tangled undergrowth. Thirty feet to our right, telltale twin trunks that shared a single canopy were actually the legs of a giant black locust bird whose plumage resembled green foliage and whose diet was the flesh of any creature foolish enough to wander beneath its "leaves."

Like a tree-sized heron, only fishing in the forest instead of shallow waters.

A few months ago, we would've unwittingly walked right beneath its savage beak. But they were easy enough to avoid if you knew what to look for.

And weren't fleeing for your life from some other beast hunting the shadows.

Ameline touched my arm. "Your turn."

We'd bound our wands to our nondominant fore-
arms so we could aim them while keeping both hands
free. It was still sort of clunky but a small enough price
to pay for having magic that might protect us. I pointed
my left arm toward my face and imagined unmasking
my second sight.

Shutting my eyes went against my instincts, but I
trusted my companions and *looked* around. A large
flicker of light confirmed my identification of the tree-
bird. Behind me, lots of small, muted flickers suggested
a large group of something nesting in the trees. Things I
hadn't spotted with my own eyes.

That left one direction that seemed clear. Or did it? I
thought there might've been the faintest flicker in that
direction too. Faint because it was weak? Far away?
Hidden somehow? Or was I just imagining things?

Somewhere in the distance, someone screamed.
Something else roared. One of the other teams had run
into trouble.

My eyes snapped open. I spared a quick prayer that
everyone would make it back safely, then returned my
focus to the one part I had any control over. My own
team.

"What do you guys see?"

Ameline answered first. "Black locust bird over
there. A troop of masked wailer monkeys in the trees
that way."

That was bad news. Masked wailer monkeys were
highly territorial. They weren't nocturnal, but it wouldn't

stop them attacking if we ventured near. And they were spread through a good half of the surrounding canopy.

"Bryn?"

"That would account for all the heat signatures I'm seeing in the vicinity too."

I wasn't confident enough in my own second sight to trust I'd seen anything in the remaining direction. "Then I guess we go this way."

Still, as a final precaution, I chose a long stick to test the ground before me. Some dangers weren't detectable by second sight. "I'll lead. You guys keep scanning."

But I'd only made it ten paces when my stick sank deep into the earth. Too deep. When I pulled it back, the end was shorter and crawling with small insects.

"Terrants," I hissed.

I hurled the stick fifteen feet in front of us as a decoy, hoping the nest would move toward it instead of us. Then I backed away with extreme care. We'd learned to tread quietly and with minimal disturbance to the forest floor in our Survival Skills class, but they'd likely still be able to locate us.

Bryn was backing up just as carefully behind me. "Their heat signatures must've been blocked by the soil."

"I still can't see them either," Ameline reported. "Or communicate with them for that matter."

I closed my eyes for a moment. The flicker was clearer this time, perhaps because I was closer. "I can see them, but only just. We better choose a different route fast."

"I can probably convince the black locust bird to move to different hunting grounds," Ameline offered.

Bryn was just as quick to volunteer. "Wilverness said they're quite flammable, so I bet I can convince it to move along."

Fire was her solution for just about everything, but the idea had merit. The black locust birds had an aversion to fire.

"How about we use a combination of both to conserve your magic? Bryn, you can light a small fire that will kick the bird's instincts into gear, and Ameline, you can play on those instincts to convince it to move."

"Spoilsport," Bryn muttered. She lifted her arm, and a small fire sprang up at the base of the twin trunks.

But I knew from her lack of further protest and the modest size of those flames that she agreed with my compromise. Conserving magic would be vital in this trial.

Ameline frowned in the bird's direction, and one of those "trunks" uprooted and stomped on the patch of flame.

It went out.

I checked the ground we'd just retreated from for terrants—employing both another stick and my second sight. The insects were advancing toward us. But slowly. Perhaps unsure of our location now we'd stopped moving.

We were safe enough for now. I let my friends concentrate on their own tasks.

"Can you light a fire halfway between us and the bird?" Ameline asked. "It might be birdbrained, but it has useful preservation instincts."

Another small leaf fire broke out. And a moment later the second "trunk" uprooted. This time it didn't stomp out the flames; it moved away instead.

The bird was so large that its first step carried it ten feet. By its third, we had enough room to dash out of the clearing.

"Nice," I said. "Let's get out of here before anything comes to investigate that fire."

*Or the terrants suck us into the earth and devour our flesh,* I added silently. At least the nasty little insects weren't particularly fast.

I led the way again, my companions forming an arrowhead formation behind me. Their superior second-sight scouting abilities provided a valid reason for me to take point, but it was the position I would've wanted anyway. If we ran face-first into danger and had no time for magic, I was best equipped to handle it.

Bryn was fearless and competent enough with her daggers, but her petite frame did her few favors when it came to fighting. My tall athletic build was better for strength and reach, and I was more practiced with a weapon. Not to mention Bryn was a tad *too* fearless to make a good leader.

And Ameline... Her magic affinity with creatures was incredibly useful. But three months at the academy had not changed the fact that she was good and gentle and kind. Too gentle and kind for the fate of the first-borns. It didn't matter that most of the beasts we dealt with were bloodthirsty monsters. Ameline wanted to live in harmony with them all. She was the only student who, despite all the trials we'd faced, had gone the entire time without resorting to bloodshed. Two things had made that possible: her affinity with creatures and my stepping ahead to do the dirty work anytime I could.

Because protecting Ameline from *physical* harm had only ever been half my ambition. I wanted to protect her wonderful, gentle soul and her warm and tender heart too.

So I would lead the way. And anything that tried to get to Ameline would have to do so over my dead body.

Not that I told her that.

Then again, it wouldn't surprise me if she already knew.

As soon as I judged we'd put sufficient distance between us and Bryn's smoking fire, we slowed to search for vinegar moss. A common species that smelled even worse than it sounded but was otherwise harmless.

Not everything hunted by sight. So we rubbed the stinking moss all over us to conceal our scents, singeing our nostrils in the process. We also strived to keep noise to a minimum, although there was only so much we could do walking on leaf litter.

We skirted the edge of a colony of hellwings, avoided the creeping snakeberry vines, and steered well clear of an embercat's den.

Then Ameline paused. "Can you smell that? Like bitter melon and rotten lime?"

In truth, I'd been trying very hard not to smell anything at all. But I sniffed the air obediently, relieved to find my nose had grown accustomed to the vinegar moss's obnoxious odor and was now filtering it out.

Sure enough, I smelled the acrid fruitiness too. Not a pleasant scent, but a distinct one, and far more agreeable than our own fragrance.

Sleepwood shrubs.

With luck, we might still be on the right side of the season to make use of their seedpods.

We'd learned about them in our botany classes—if burst while still green, they released toxic spores that caused instant paralysis in anything that inhaled them. They were a last-resort kind of measure because if the wind changed at the wrong moment, you'd be the one lying helpless on the forest floor. And your target—who was likely bigger and nastier than you—was also likely to regain function of its limbs before you did.

Still, we may yet need a last resort tonight.

We checked the area for night crawler spiders, which fed on the sap of the same plants to sharpen their venom and often made their lairs nearby. Even with our second sight, the coast looked clear. So we scoured the shrubs and found two seedpods still green enough to work.

The seedpods were oblong and as large as coconuts, making them awkward to carry without piercing the hard shell. But Bryn and I cut a strip of fabric from our cloaks and tied them to our belts.

We'd barely progressed another fifty yards when Bryn cursed quietly. "Something very large and hot enough to breathe fire is coming in at two o'clock."

Ameline squinted in that direction, trying to identify the threat.

She blanched. "A shadow stalker. Start climbing!"

Shadow stalkers were a vicious fusion of dragon, leopard, and dinosaur and had the reputation of being one of the most lethal predators in the forest.

Even if we somehow survived an encounter, we'd be drained and defenseless and never make it back. There were too many miles of dark and dangerous forest between us and safety.

So we dashed to the nearest climbable trunk and scrambled upward. The monsters hunted by sight and smell, but their hearing was relatively weak and they were too heavy for tree climbing. Which meant if we could ascend high into the branches and stay very, very still, we might just escape its notice.

"Incoming," Bryn warned.

We froze where we were.

A second later, the shadow stalker prowled into view.

Its dark body was long and sleek with four powerful legs that moved with leopard-like grace and speed. Impenetrable armored plating and squat, razor-sharp spikes covered its back—which was too close to our hiding spot for comfort—the spikes lengthening into increasingly dangerous weapons the closer they came to its head. The head itself bore the ferocious reptilian characteristics of a dragon and was equally capable of breathing fire. And as if that wasn't enough, the monster had a brutal club tail we'd been told it could wield with bone-breaking accuracy.

From terrifying head to equally terrifying tail, it was about thirty feet long, though its club tail made up half of that.

All we could do was stay frozen and hope the leaves we'd rubbed into our skin would conceal our scent, hope that we'd climbed high enough, and hope none of us would be overcome by the sudden urge to sneeze.

If it saw or smelled us, it would burn down the tree or smash the trunk into splinters with its tail.

The monster moved with impossible quietness for a creature so large, advancing through the undergrowth with barely a rustle. We held our breath and prayed it would not look up.

It stopped beneath our tree, nostrils flaring.

Cold dread trickled through me. Curse the fates, we had not survived all these months at the academy just to become this thing's meal.

The giant beast resumed prowling, and after its tail receded from view, I resumed breathing too. But we still didn't move. Still didn't count ourselves safe yet.

Shadow stalkers always hunted in pairs.

A long, long minute passed before the second one appeared.

It was larger than the first, closer to our hideout. Its spikes glinted wickedly in the moonlight. This stalker too paused beneath our tree. Just in case our frantic hearts hadn't had enough of a workout.

But it moved on.

We waited another five long minutes, Bryn and Ameline making sure the stalkers were well out of range before we returned to the earth. My limbs had gone weak with relief—which wasn't ideal when I was relying on them to convey me down the trunk.

That had been close.

We resumed our cautious journey through the forest.

I was leading the way after an uneventful half mile when Ameline shrieked.

I spun to see her airborne. Grasped in the creepy fingerlike feet of a giant bat crossed with something more nightmarish.

I leaped at Ameline's trailing legs. The bat thing was big, but could it carry both of us?

Apparently it could.

But as much as the leathery wings labored, we were no longer gaining height. Instead, we were being swept along, five feet off the forest floor, our legs tangling occasionally with the undergrowth. I freed my dagger from its sheath.

Ameline had recovered from the shock and had her

wand arm aimed at the creature. Whatever she was trying didn't seem to be working. A fireball smacked into its back from where Bryn was racing below, singeing the scattering of fur there and worsening the already unpleasant musty odor. The bat thing screeched but did not release us.

Until I hauled myself upward and hacked off its foot.

We tumbled to the earth together and landed in unkind shrubbery.

It hurt less than falling off a tower anyway.

"You okay?" I asked.

I was hoping the crashing sounds growing nearer was Bryn and not some new predator.

Ameline didn't look so good. Her skin was scratched by the bushes that had broken our fall; her complexion was white and her eyes wide.

I mistook the cause of her fear.

"Fine," she said. "But look. Are those night crawler threads?"

Fine silken threads were strung all around us, barely visible in the gloom. We'd found another patch of sleep-wood shrubs. And these were already claimed.

I closed my eyes, just for a moment, and saw hundreds of faint flickers.

Night crawlers did not hunt like normal spiders. Their webs were not hung to catch their prey but as the sensors of an alarm system that detected when a meal had been gracious enough to wander into their hunting ground.

They were also the size of rabbits and hunted in force.

"Run," I hissed, just as the frontline of the night crawler army scuttled into view.

Ameline and I ran, calling out to Bryn as we did. But we weren't running in terror. Well, not *just* terror anyway. We were running toward the flowing water we could hear down the slope.

Night crawlers hated water. So that was where we'd make our stand.

Amazing how much information you could retain when your life depended on it.

Of course, we had to make it to the river first. The spiders were rushing after us in a swarm so large they looked like thick, viscous fluid flowing down the hill.

Somewhere off to the side, Bryn was fighting to join us.

The night crawlers were going to reach us first.

But the river was in sight now. And so was Bryn. She was running—downhill from the encroaching landslide of leggy, venomous arachnids, yet with more distance to go.

Then Ameline went down. Hard. Her foot catching on a concealed root and sending her sprawling facedown into the leaf litter.

Heart in my throat, I skidded to a stop and dashed

back up the hill in a race to prevent the oncoming horde from burying her alive with their furry bodies.

Bryn saved us both. A wall of flame erupted a bare six inches from where Ameline was shoving herself to her feet.

The swarm shrank from the fire.

I lunged to help Ameline up. The flames were already dwindling. I couldn't imagine how much of Bryn's power that had drained.

We ran, Ameline limping now, my arm around her waist, trying to lend what support I could. Behind us, the wall of flames went out.

The horde resumed its hunt.

We reached the water's edge and spun to face the oncoming throng. The river was too wide to leap across, and Wilverness had warned us that *worse* things lived in the forest's waters. Warned us not to dip so much as a toe into any waterway we came across.

But the spiders would avoid it too, effectively giving them only one direction to attack us from.

Thanks to her wall of flame, Bryn reached us half a second before the first wave of night crawlers did. Without needing to confer, we took up position on either side of Ameline. She was far more effective using her magic than she was a blade.

Then the swarm hit.

I kicked the forerunner into the one behind it, feeling its soft abdomen splatter against my boot, and stomped on the next, which left, oh, about a dozen jumping and racing up my legs, biting as they went. I'd already drawn both my daggers, which made short work of the immediate encroachers, along with those that had slipped past me to Ameline.

Ameline's wand arm was stretched outward, her attention fixed in the distance where the rear half of the horde had stopped. She was holding them back.

Bryn was focused on those closer to us, setting the leaf litter on fire beneath them and stomping and swiping at any that broke through.

But any we killed were replaced with a dozen more.

I poured magical speed into my limbs. I didn't have an affinity, but I'd found enhancing my physical capacities was an efficient way of using my power. I slashed and stabbed and kicked and stomped until I was slipping in spider guts.

They kept coming.

The night crawler venom was taking hold, turning my limbs increasingly numb. Not paralyzed, not like the sleepwood seedpods. But the lack of feeling was making me clumsy, making me fumble. And I could no longer feel the skitter of legs up my pants and over my back or the needle-like fangs sinking into my flesh.

Their venom wasn't deadly. Just incapacitating. Because night crawlers liked to keep their prey alive while they feasted on it.

Sometimes over multiple days.

The venom prevented their victims from going into

shock and dying, and the spiders' saliva prevented them from bleeding out.

The crawlers wanted their meals fresh and warm.

Now would've been an excellent time to use one of our last-resort seedpods. Except thanks to the night crawlers symbiotic relationship with sleepwood shrubs, they were one of the few creatures immune to the spores' effects. That, and the wind would blow it straight back in our faces anyway.

So we fought on.

I dropped one of my daggers and couldn't find it again in the mess of slime and bodies at my feet. I punched or threw or slapped instead.

Bryn must have run out of fire or sufficient fuel because she'd switched to fighting purely with her own weapons too.

Ameline was still holding back over half the horde, sweat beading on her forehead from the effort.

At this rate, it wouldn't matter.

Then something splashed behind me, the hair stood up on the back of my neck, and as one, the spiders turned and fled.

It was not Ameline's doing.

Heart thudding in my ears, I swiveled to see what had made them run.

# CHAPTER 27

An elemental was rising from the river in the watery likeness of a woman.

The figure towered over us, so large it had lowered the level of the river to build its current shape. Watery hair hung long and loose, and a flowing dress was formed from thick, swirling ribbons of more tightly controlled water.

Without taking my eyes off the creature, I aimed my wand at the ground beneath us and buried our boots in the soil before setting it like concrete.

Then the elemental struck. Too late I realized the long, twisting rivulets I'd mistaken for a dress were tentacles. They smashed into us with the force of a wave, grabbing us and sucking at us, trying to pull us into the river.

Our feet held firm.

But as the water slapped and splashed around me, I began to wonder if we could drown standing upright on supposedly dry land.

My dagger was useless against a being of water. Bryn dredged up the spark of a fire that was instantly drenched. And though Ameline's arm was pointed at the elemental's head, the assault kept coming.

Ameline's affinity could steer and leverage the natural instincts of many creatures. But her level of influence was affected by the power and intelligence of the other entity. She could still attempt to communicate with greater beings through images and sensations, but the elemental would find it easy to ignore her. And it was doing just that.

Even so, and luckily for us, the thing did not make a concerted effort to drown us on dry land. Instead, realizing that water alone could not tug our anchored feet free, the elemental solidified.

The watery likeness of a head morphed to one that possessed real skin, eyes, and hair the color of a dark stagnant pool. The liquid tentacles hardened into wet flesh complete with suction cups. And this time, when they wrapped around us, they did it with near bone-crushing force.

The elemental was more formidable now, more real. But it was also something we could fight.

I found enough breath in my lungs to gasp, "On the count of three, we strike together. Three. Two. One."

Bryn seared the now able-to-be-burned flesh.

I poured strength and speed into my arms and hacked off the tentacle around my waist, then caught and stabbed the one that swung at my head.

Ameline blasted the elemental with a mental attack that made the tentacles recoil. Only for a moment. But that was enough.

I made the ground spit us out, and we used that moment to dash out of reach.

The elemental emitted a gurgling shriek of thwarted intent and plunged back into the river with the crashing thunder of a waterfall.

We stopped thirty yards from the bank and took a few minutes to recollect ourselves. We were trembling with shock and exhaustion, and none of us had much to say.

I retrieved a third dagger from the extra sheath on my lower leg. I'd learned how liable I was to lose them and brought a backup blade for this trial. Just as well, it seemed. Though Bryn had managed to hang on to both of hers. We also splinted Ameline's twisted ankle, the numbness from the crawler's venom making the fiddly task difficult.

When the shakiness had subsided and our labored breathing returned to normal, we pushed on.

For the next mile we hid, fled, and tricked our way past a series of monsters. We weren't trying to be heroes. We just wanted to make it to safety.

Every one of us was weary, limping, and almost completely drained of magic by the time we saw the brilliant lights of the academy shining through the trees. I couldn't afford to lose my night vision, so I only glanced at the welcome sight before returning my gaze to our immediate surroundings. Even from afar, the sentinel hedge cats were visible, standing out in stark relief against the bright backdrop.

I knew better than to relax until we crossed that invisible line, but I felt the stirrings of relief all the same.

Until Grimwort emerged through a short-distance gateway to block our route.

"Congratulations," he said with the enthusiasm of a kid on toilet-cleaning duty. "You've almost completed your final trial. But since no true mission goes to plan, you have one last challenge to overcome."

Then the bastard opened a gateway beneath our feet.

We fell through it. Landing somewhere else entirely. Trees still surrounded us, stretching high overhead, but they were not the ones I was used to seeing. That together with the three inches of snow on the ground told me we'd traveled a great distance in one fleeting moment.

Which meant we were now far, far from safety.

Too far. A distance untraversable by foot. Especially in our current condition with no supplies.

More snow was drifting from the sky, but my eyes landed on an old runegate in the middle of a clearing. A glowing runegate. Through its archway, I could see the inviting expanse of Millicent's lawn.

But no relief washed over me.

Because prowling between us and our only way home were two lethal shadow stalkers.

And this time there would be no way to hide.

# CHAPTER 28

Fear spiked through me. Followed by anger. Followed by more of both.

But I pushed my anger at the walkers deep down where I stored the rest of it. Anger for the destruction of our world. For the slaughter—directly and indirectly— of billions of human lives. For the sorrow and sacrifice and grief and pain of the Firstborn Agreement. For all the families that had been broken, never to be whole again. For my father, sister, brother, and mother who I'd been torn from forever. For draining Fletcher of the warmth and light that had once defined him. For forcing Ameline into situation after situation that threatened to darken her soul too. For putting our lives so needlessly at risk in this trial. Even for poor Jayden who should've lived out his coddled existence within the overindulgent arms of his family.

Now was not the time to channel that anger.

But that time would come.

I'd make sure of it.

However, to do that, I first had to make sure my friends and I survived.

A task that seemed impossible. We were magically and physically spent. The runegate was in the center of a giant clearing that started just fifteen yards down the forested slope we were standing on. Which meant there would be no trees to climb this time. No cover of any kind. And there was zero chance we could sprint the eighty yards across the clearing to the runegate without the shadow stalkers running us down.

The beasts were showing no sign of moving on either. In fact, they were behaving unusually. Like they were guarding the runegate.

Or like they knew we were coming. That if they only waited, we'd save them the trouble of the hunt and serve ourselves up to them.

To finish it all off, the below-freezing weather meant we didn't have much time to plan.

In short, we were royally screwed.

Unless…

The sleepwood seedpods.

If there was ever a time of last resort, this was it.

I checked the wind's direction. Perhaps our luck was finally about to change. So long as the wind didn't.

Working slowly so as not to draw the stalkers' gaze with rapid movement, I cut the seedpod I was carrying from my belt. My hands were too numb from the night crawler venom to bother fumbling with the fabric ties.

I suspected if they hadn't been numb, they would've been hurting from the cold. But if this succeeded, we were less than a hundred yards from home.

"If I lob this close, do either of you have enough magic left to crack it open?"

Ameline nodded. "I do."

"Great." I checked the wind again. Still blowing toward the shadow stalkers and away from us.

Lucky it was only a faint breeze since that meant we were upwind. I wasn't sure how well our vinegar moss perfume would be holding up after our encounter with the water elemental and the sweating we'd done before and since.

In any case, it didn't need to hold up much longer.

I eased myself down the slope to find a vantage to throw from. My friends followed just as cautiously. When I stopped, Ameline surveyed the nearby trunks.

"If this doesn't work, we'd better be prepared to climb fast."

"Good point." I located a good climbing tree just to my left, then sent a tiny trickle of magical strength down my right arm. I was usually a good throw, but with so much riding on this, I was worried.

I checked my friends were ready, checked the wind a final time, and threw the seedpod into the clearing.

My aim was near perfect. It hit the ground ten feet

in front of the closer shadow stalker, bounced once, and came to a stop.

The monster snapped its head around.

Ameline aimed her wand arm, and the seedpod broke in half.

Maybe the shadow stalker recognized the threat for what it was. Or maybe it was the beast's go-to method for dealing with any unknown, but it unleashed a torrent of flame from its dragon-like jaws. When the flames cleared, nothing but ash remained.

We held our breath. Not because we worried the spores would reach us but because we were hoping that despite the miniature firestorm, they might yet reach the nearest shadow stalker.

Nothing happened.

Apparently the flame had incinerated or neutralized the paralyzing spores.

I closed my eyes for a few seconds, failure and cold and fatigue dragging at me, willing me to lie down and give up. I kept my eyes closed a moment longer so my friends wouldn't see my despair.

Our last resort had failed.

I tried to rally myself. I was *not* going to stand here on the perimeter of this damn clearing, so close to safety, and die of exposure.

Despite the fire show, the shadow stalkers were showing no sign of hunting us down. They were sticking close to the runegate.

"Ameline, can you communicate with them?"

She shook her head. "No. I think… it's like their minds have been messed with. They're protecting the runegate like it's a third life mate. And they're operating on pure instinct. Furious instinct."

Fabulous.

Shadow stalkers were notoriously protective of their life mates. If you messed with one, you'd better be prepared to deal with the wrath of both.

Oddly enough, they were far less attached to their offspring.

"All right." I temporized. "You stay back and do what you can to mentally distract them whenever we need help."

Ameline bit her lip. We both knew the shadow stalkers were no mere night crawlers. That if Bryn and I walked into that clearing, we probably wouldn't return. But I turned my back on my childhood friend before she could object.

I shifted to focus on Bryn, to learn whether her bravado, her sense of adventure, her reckless courage was somehow still with her. Whether she would go with me into battle. I could use a dose of her feisty, irrepressible spirit right now. "How do you want to—"

Except she wasn't there.

She was running. Down the slope. Into the clearing. Toward the shadow stalkers.

What the hell?

Then I saw the item she was concealing from the

monsters and realized what she must be intending. Behind her back, she clutched the second seedpod.

Bryn was planning to take down one of the stalkers. And she would take down herself with it.

At first the nearest shadow stalker only stared. Too stunned to react—like I was.

Her plan, her running off without consulting us first, only made sense if she didn't intend for us to tackle the second monster. Which could mean only one thing.

She was sacrificing herself to bring down one of the shadow stalkers in the hope that its life mate would be so distracted that Ameline and I could reach the runegate.

I would never have expected Bryn to do something like this. She was street-smart, independent, and she put herself first. She'd had to do that to survive her upbringing. It didn't mean she didn't care about anyone else. She did. I'd seen that. But this was something else altogether. She was throwing her life away for Ameline's and mine.

The shadow stalker recovered from the shock faster than I did.

Bryn, who was getting close, slowed to a casual walk. Probably trying to encourage the beast to eat her rather than incinerate her.

The shadow stalker lifted its head to catch her scent, then dashed forward.

"No!" The word tore from my throat.

And then I was running too. Already knowing that I was too late to save her.

Time slowed to a crawl.

I watched in horror as the monster bore down on my friend. It was so enormous that it would take just two bites to devour her.

Only one to kill her.

The reptilian head reared back in preparation to strike, the fearsome maw opening wide to reveal long rows of serrated teeth.

Bryn waited until that moment to slam a blade into the seedpod and hack it open.

Time slowed further, crawling now like a dying insect dragging itself over viscous mud.

The giant head snaked toward her.

She tried to throw the seedpod to meet it, but she was already swaying from the spores' effects.

The seedpod slipped from her fingers and tumbled to the snow.

Bryn and the shadow stalker followed an instant later. Only luck and inches preventing the monster from crushing her beneath its weight.

Time snapped back.

The paralyzed stalker's life mate let out a cry that rent the air before it charged into action. Vengeance.

That was when I realized Ameline was running beside me.

"Stay back," I snapped. "I can't protect you both!"

But she didn't stop running. And despite her injured ankle, she was almost keeping up.

Her jaw was set. "Getting yourself killed isn't

protecting me, you idiot! Having you around will always be more important for my well-being than anything else."

Geez. Her words hit me like a physical blow.

"Give me a weapon," she demanded.

There was no time to argue. I gave her the dagger already in my hand.

But I did find a moment to feel guilty for committing the same sin as everyone else. For underestimating Ameline.

For underestimating Bryn too.

It only made me more determined to save them...

The second shadow stalker was barreling toward Bryn and its mate. I sprinted to intercept it.

The sleepwood paralysis did not knock you unconscious. She was lying there completely aware of what was happening. Of what she was sacrificing. Of her imminent death. And she was unable to move so much as a finger to prevent it.

Tears I did not have the liberty for blurred my vision.

*Dammit, Bryn. What a time to choose to become a martyr.*

I'd started running without a plan. Now I had one, but it wasn't much of one.

Wilverness had taught us the only place where heavily armored shadow stalkers could be taken down with an ordinary weapon. It was just impossible to get to. Tiny ear holes located way up on the side of their giant snake-necked, sharp-toothed, fire-breathing heads.

The shadow stalker saw me coming and veered to meet me.

I dashed right, felt its jaws snap inches from my back, and flung myself at its leg. This particular specimen was about the size of a bus. But the armored plates, which would deflect almost any weapon, also provided something to cling to.

My arms all but wrenched from their sockets as the beast's momentum met mine. But it was slowing to turn and charge after me, and all that exercise on the tower trial and under Cricklewood's tutelage had done me some good, because I didn't let go.

Instead, I clambered my way up to its knee and then its shoulder. And then I was on its back. There was just enough room between the spikes for the width of my body.

I flattened myself to its armored ridges as the sledge-hammer of a tail swung at me, the force of its passing whipping my hair around my face as it missed me by a mere inch.

Crap. I hadn't counted on that complication.

The shadow stalker evidently did not appreciate me on its back. It bucked and spun, and it was all I could do to hold on, then flatten myself again as the tail took another swing.

I had to get out of range. But the tail was long. Maybe there was no such thing as out of range.

I scrambled toward the beast's head. The spikes on its back grew longer and more closely packed as I inched toward its neck. Dodging them as well as the swinging tail while holding on for dear life was going to be problematic.

The next time the sledgehammer tail whipped around, I dodged a fraction of a second too late and it caught the back of my left ankle. Pain exploded on impact. Probably bone too. And if it weren't for the remaining numbness from the damn night crawlers, I might've blacked out.

Instead, I dragged myself toward the creature's neck, staying low and keeping as much of myself pressed against the shadow stalker as I could.

Ameline was on the ground, yelling and waving her arms, trying to split the beast's attention between her and me and definitely not Bryn, who lay motionless in the snow.

To my relief, the stalker seemed more preoccupied with me than either of them. I hauled myself forward another few inches. Those neck spikes now represented safety. It wouldn't be able to wield its tail against me if I could squeeze between those longer spines. Not unless it was prepared to damage itself to get to me.

I grasped the blunted base of the first spine. The point was sharp, but the lower half I could grip without cutting myself. My other hand wrapped around the next one, and I used them to haul myself up its neck like some sort of dangerous playground equipment.

That was when the stalker slammed its head up and back. Driving one of those spikes into my gut.

I screamed. The sound went on far longer than I wanted it to. And time slowed for a second instance.

I saw Ameline's eyes widen in horror. Then narrow with something else altogether.

I saw that Bryn's face was now dusted with snow that was still falling from the sky. The image oddly peaceful in the roaring pain and chaos and the blackness encroaching at the edges of my vision.

And I saw that I was now only two feet from the shallow indentation that indicated the ear hole. My target.

I shoved myself off the spike.

My front was cold and hot and wet and numb and on agonizing, endless fire all at once.

But my friends were relying on me. My friends who were risking their own lives for mine. And dammit to hell if I would let the walkers win.

I forced my leaden limbs to move. It was like slogging through cold molasses. Only with more pain and a violent, bucking beast beneath you.

Ameline ran forward screaming a war cry—armed only with a useless dagger, her ineffectual wand, and a love greater than I could bear.

I dragged myself another foot.

The stalker's attention was—momentarily—fixed on Ameline. Its body briefly still as it calculated how best to kill her.

My own limbs were trembling. With pain or blood loss or fear and fury for my friends, I did not know. But I made that moment count. I forced myself across that last seemingly insurmountable distance, grasped my remaining dagger from its sheath, and sent the last trickle of energy I had into my right arm.

The edges of my vision darkened further. Unconsciousness beckoning.

I felt rather than saw the shadow stalker's muscles bunch beneath me as it prepared to snap Ameline in half.

I struck first. Driving the dagger into its ear and hoping desperately the weapon would be long enough to reach its brain.

The blade bit deep, sinking all the way to the hilt. And the shadow stalker toppled. Only thirty feet from its fallen partner.

From Bryn.

The impact of the ground against my mortal injuries turned my world completely black.

Sheer determination forced my eyes to open, and the edges of that blackness receded slightly.

I had to know.

Ameline's tear-stricken face swam into view. "Don't you dare die on me, or I'll tell everyone you were killed by a bush turkey. Is that what you want?"

I cracked a smile. Hell's breath, it hurt. Everything hurt. But I managed to croak out the question I needed answered.

"Bryn?"

"She's okay. I'll bring her over here to stop your bleeding. Hang on."

I rolled my head to watch. Ameline ran the ten yards to Bryn and leaned down to say something. Beside them, the paralyzed shadow stalker twitched.

The effects of the sleepwood spores were wearing off.

A fresh wave of fear coursed through me. But even the fear was weak now. All I could focus on was the pain. The cold blackness sucking me in and downward.

I tried to call out a warning, but my voice had stopped working. Everything was stopping working.

Ameline had seen the twitch though. She stood up, retrieved the borrowed dagger from wherever she'd stashed it, and slammed the blade into the beast's ear. Just like that. Her expression was grim, but she spared no tears for the slain stalker. For what she'd just done.

Through the miasma of pain, distant but unmistakable, I recognized my shock. My sorrow at the loss of her innocence. My pride at her courage and pragmatism.

Then she dragged Bryn over to me and propped her into a sitting position. Bryn, still paralyzed, her eyes unable to so much as blink, dredged up the last of her magic to cauterize the hole in my gut. To put an end to the flow of lifeblood pumping from my body and staining the snow red.

Real fire collided with the blaze of agony already there. I smelled burning meat. And surrendered at last to the darkness.

# CHAPTER 29

I woke on the other side of the runegate. In the infirmary.

The beds were full.

The glass ceiling showed it was still dark outside, but soft yellow light illuminated Invermoore's workspace.

The healer must have labored through the night. Her stern face was drawn, her gray eyes clouded with fatigue, and the state of her hair and clothes an utter mess by walker standards.

But while I ached all over, my formerly shattered ankle was whole and my stomach barely hurt any more than the rest of me.

Bryn was stretched out in the bed beside mine. I'd never been more delighted to hear her gentle snores.

Later I learned that she'd pushed herself into unconsciousness to stop my bleeding. To keep me alive long enough for Ameline to drag us both through the runegate to safety. A Herculean task in itself.

Later I learned I'd been branded forever by that final trial. Not just the scars on my skin, but the marks left on my heart by what my friends had been willing to sacrifice for me.

But right then all I felt was relief.

We'd done it. Survived the three months. Completed the final trial. Not everyone could say the same.

Some would never say anything again.

Now we just had to hope it would be enough…

I closed my eyes to snatch a few last hours of sleep before we learned our fates.

# CHAPTER 30

Ameline came to collect us. The sky above the glass ceiling was streaked with gray. Almost dawn.

"They're posting the lists in a few minutes. Are you well enough to walk?"

Was I? Around me, many of the beds had emptied, and other kids were rising from their mattresses or waiting for their beds to be lowered so they could leave too. A few remained unmoving. Too injured to wake. The comatose boy from another year's intake of firstborns somewhere among them.

Bryn shoved her blankets back. "Hell yes. I'm not going to miss this."

A large bruise covered her left cheek, and her usually golden complexion had an ashy pallor to it, but her eyes sparked with determination. Ameline looked worse for wear too, like she'd spent the night tossing and turning alone in the room she normally shared with us. Perhaps wondering if we'd made it through till dawn. Her blond halo was mussed and dull and the circles beneath her eyes purple.

I was sure I wasn't about to win any beauty contests either. If they were handing out prizes for zombie costumes, however…

I pushed off my blankets and struggled into a sitting position. The three of us had been through hell together, and we would face whatever was coming side by side too. My friends were strong. Stronger even than I'd given them credit for. But we were stronger together.

We probably didn't look it though as we forced our unwilling bodies to trudge through Millicent's corridors. The journey to the dining hall had never felt so long.

When we reached it, Dunraven was departing and a sea of kids were clustering around one section of the wall.

We had to wait our turn. I swayed on my feet, and Ameline steadied me.

Our classmates' expressions when they turned away from the wall were confused, cautious, like they still weren't sure of the outcome. Yet they left the dining hall with purpose.

Then it was our turn.

Two lists of names written in the same graceful script were stuck to the wall on ordinary sheets of paper. So mundane for objects upon which the courses of our lives would turn.

There was no indication which list was which. Of

who had passed and who had failed. But one list of names was noticeably longer than the other.

I scanned the shorter list as fast as I could, needing to know and figuring this was the quickest way of finding out. Klay's was on top, which probably meant this was the one we wanted to be on. I saw my own name first. *Nova.* Bryn's name was six down from mine. Heart in my throat, I kept scanning.

And scanning.

And scanning.

And there, right at the bottom, was the third name I'd desperately wanted to find. *Ameline.*

"We're on the same list!"

We whooped and hugged and carried on like excited eight-year-olds. Very stiff and sore excited eight-year-olds anyway.

We would be sticking together. I was so relieved that I almost didn't care *which* group we were in. Those that would stay or those that would depart immediately.

But no, that wasn't true. I did care. I wanted to win. In part because we'd worked so hard for this. In part because we still had no idea what happened to those who failed. And in part because staying at the academy was a far better position to destroy it from.

At least we didn't have long to wait. Beneath our names were instructions for all the students listed above to make their way to one of the bigger classrooms. The kids on the second list were directed to go to the largest tower room.

We gathered in the specified classroom, my body gladly sinking into one of the seats, and waited to learn what our future would hold.

Professor Grimwort was already there. Apparently he would be the one to deliver the news. Was that a good sign or bad?

He waited up front for everyone to trickle in and then be seated and silent before talking. Or perhaps he was aware of how taut our nerves were and was enjoying screwing with us.

"If you are in this room, you have been deemed the strongest, fittest, most skilled, and magically gifted among your human peers. Congratulations."

His words were congratulatory. His tone was not. But despite that and the chilling details we'd uncovered about the transformation ritual, I felt a surge of triumph.

We had made it! All three of us had defeated the odds, overcome everything the professors had thrown in our path, and demonstrated our strength, skill, and resilience.

Only a third of the original students had managed the same.

"In short," Grimwort was saying, "you have distinguished yourselves as the most suitable candidates for this academy's ultimate purpose."

My curiosity spiked. I'd been trying to figure out what was really going on here since I'd first arrived. Maybe they would finally tell us.

"Which is…" Grimwort paused. He had our complete attention. "To form and train a specialized contingent of elite warriors."

My brain churned over the revelation. Given the content of our classes over the past three months, it wasn't a complete shock. Yet it made zero sense in the context of reality as I understood it.

Who would we be fighting? The walkers already ruled the world.

Someone else asked the question aloud. "Sir, who or what will this contingent be fighting against?"

Grimwort glowered at the interruption. "You'll find that out soon enough. The question that should've occurred to you is why the walkers would bother training humans to be part of this warrior unit."

Ding, ding, ding. That's exactly what I was wondering. We might be the best of the best among the human students. But the weakest walker—even stooped and ancient Cricklewood or the pixie-like girl shorter than Bryn who spent most of her lessons magically altering her hair color to alarming hues—would beat us in any sort of fair fight. Most unfair fights too.

Were they that desperate for soldiers?

But if we were here to be cannon fodder—a distraction for the enemy to play with while the walker troops moved into position—why kick out two-thirds of the students?

Unless…

Anxiety crept over me. Unless the "enemy" was

humankind. Unless they needed our insight or ability to blend in or—

But no. That didn't make sense either. Not unless the rich and powerful humans that fled fifty years ago were coming back equipped with something so powerful I couldn't conceive it. The timing didn't work regardless. The Agreement had come into place thirty-seven years ago. Surely if a war had been waging all that time between the humans that fled and the walkers that had taken over, we'd know about it.

Grimwort cleared his throat to silence the whispers of speculation.

"If we left you in your natural state, you would indeed be useless to us. Which is why, before we begin the next phase of your training, each student in this room will undergo a transformation ritual. The ritual itself is not without risk, but assuming you survive, it will unlock great power beyond the conception of most of your kind."

This time the hum of speculation was louder. A mixture of shock and nerves and excitement.

The excitement seemed to be winning out. Our classmates hadn't seen the creepy transformation chamber. Or the changes in my old friend.

"Those of you here are the strongest of your cohort both mentally and physically. That gives you a superior chance of surviving the transformation. Even so, it is best that you prepare your bodies for the ordeal." Grimwort swept his hawklike gaze over the captive audience.

"From the time you leave this room until sundown three days hence, you will be excused from all academy activities. You will fast, drinking only the precious revitalizing nectar you'll receive from Glenn and Glennys. Endeavor to prepare your minds as well. Do whatever you must to find peace. It may be the difference between dying and coming through the transformation process. Healer Invermoore will come for you when it is your time."

Grimwort took a step toward the exit, then halted. Turned back.

"Those of you that survive will begin the advanced training next week and receive the answers to your remaining questions then."

The professor disappeared out the door, and the buzz of conversation turned into a roar.

# CHAPTER 31

Bryn, Ameline, and I headed for our dormitory where we could dissect the news in private.

The students on the second list never came out of the tower room.

The corridors felt empty with the human population reduced by two-thirds. The walkers now outnumbered us three to one.

What had happened to those who'd disappeared? Or *departed* as Glennys had put it when we'd collected a dose of the nectar.

Misty had been on that list. The girl who'd mistaken the groundbeast's lure for a flum. William, who'd had the unfortunate claim to fame of setting his desk on fire. Twice. Zoe, who'd started as the slowest endurance runner in Cricklewood's class and ended up fitter than Bryn. Noah, who we'd saved from going into the forest with Jayden.

Each of them had come here to protect their families. They'd tried and trained and survived. And now? My plan had focused on saving future firstborns from being sacrificed to uphold the Agreement. But what about the current year's kids? Or the previous ones?

If I ever succeeded in bringing the Agreement to its knees, I would try to find them. Try to return them to their families. If they still lived. But I couldn't do anything for them now.

I forced myself to focus on the present, the positive.

Bryn, Ameline, and I had defied the odds and made it through together. And whatever was coming next, we'd get through that together too.

Even if at the moment we could barely walk.

We reached our dorm room, and Millicent let us in with the lightest of pinpricks.

Theus was waiting inside.

He was standing by the window. At some point in the past few months we'd pulled aside the heavy burgundy drapes and left them there so we could enjoy the view. The forest did not hold the same level of fear over us as it once had.

Theus was apparently enjoying the view too, but he turned as we entered. His posture was casual, relaxed, nonthreatening. The expression on his beautiful face friendly.

That meant nothing. A walker could change in an instant. Could slit your throat while still smiling casually. And though he'd never lifted a finger against me, had in fact saved my and other human lives on multiple occasions, Theus was the most dangerous of all. Because sometimes, just for an instant here and there, I'd begun to feel safe in his presence.

Walkers could not be trusted.

Not that I feared he would kill me. If he'd wanted me dead, all he would've had to do was stand back and watch during that first trial. I would've died trying to save everybody. And if he'd wanted the pleasure of killing me himself, he'd had ample opportunity that night he'd caught me snooping.

But if he was playing the long game like I was, the fallout would be spectacular.

I must keep my guard up.

Except I was so incredibly weary just then that my guard was weak. Weak enough to notice the way the sunlight from the window danced over the handsome lines of his face and lit up those unfathomable deep green eyes.

Ameline told me he'd been the one to carry me to the infirmary after our final trial. Part of me wished I'd been awake for it.

The other part of me had had enough.

After the roller coaster ride of the last twelve hours, my emotions were all over the place. Desire, shock, confusion, irritation, and curiosity rushed through me.

Irritation won.

"What are you doing here?" I demanded.

*And why had Millicent let him in?*

One of Theus's expressive eyebrows lifted at my tone. "Lirielle and I thought you might have questions."

I snorted. "What, and you couldn't wait outside? How'd you get in?"

His lips quirked. "Those weren't the sorts of questions I had in mind."

I tamped down my irritation as what he was really offering penetrated my tired skull. Answers. There was nothing I was hungrier for right now.

Except maybe sleep. My body was pushing me toward my bed, but I remained standing.

Ameline and Bryn stood with me. I glanced at them, and they both nodded. We all wanted answers.

I leaned my back against the wall to hold myself upright and wondered where to start.

Bryn jumped in first. "I've got one. How does this transformation ritual work exactly, and why do you need such a creepy room to do it in?"

Theus's dark eyebrows rose again. Both of them this time. "You know about that?"

"You're the only one who's volunteered to answer questions here."

Theus inclined his head. "True enough. All right. As Grimwort has covered in Rudimentary Magic, a lot of power is carried in the blood. And as basic biology teaches, blood is vital and almost omnipresent within the body, its influence reaching far and wide."

Yes, I'd come close to learning exactly *how* vital my blood was last night.

"So the ritual uses a blood exchange and complex, ancient ceremonial magic to transform yours into something more powerful."

My brain caught on two words. "Blood exchange? What exactly do you mean by that?"

Theus considered us. Perhaps wondering whether to tell us the truth or fabricate something more palatable.

"You won't be awake for it. A healer will place you in a deep sleep, and then during the course of the ritual, your blood will be drained out, circulated through a walker's veins, and then given back to you."

Oh, and that wasn't the least bit creepy.

A new idea occurred to me. "Wait, who do we do this exchange with? The walker students? Will we be linked to them in some way?"

Like giant blood-controlled puppets, I was thinking.

But Theus shook his head. "No, they'll bring other walkers in just for the ritual. The students aren't suitable."

"Why not?"

A strange expression passed over Theus's face. One I'd never seen before. If I didn't know better, I'd call it haunted. "Have you not heard the professors call us hollows? Each walker student underwent a similar transformation ritual before we arrived."

"To make you more powerful?"

"To make us harder to kill," he corrected.

"You seem plenty difficult to kill already," I

observed. "So why do you need humans? Will the ritual make us as powerful as your average walker?"

That at least would make sense. A convenient supply of powerful soldiers they didn't have to breed themselves.

But Theus shut down the notion. "Not usually, no. In most cases, the transfer simply enhances a human's natural affinity. Think of it like concentrating the magic already in your blood. In that one area of affinity, you may be more powerful than an average walker, but your ability to perform magic outside of it will be weak at best, often nonexistent. However, for one in fifty cases, the results are unpredictable. To borrow a human term, they're like wildcards. For those outliers, the outcome is random. Their magic might be extinguished, remain untouched, change to a completely different affinity, or transform into power of a type and magnitude that even walkerkind have never seen."

I was unimpressed. Maybe to some extent because I still didn't *have* an affinity that I was aware of. And sure, the incredible wildcard power was fun to imagine, but by Theus's account, half the wildcards ended up with less power rather than more.

"So by that reckoning," I summarized, "at least forty-nine out of fifty students walk out with powers that will never match up to a walker's. That's not accounting for the ones that never walk out at all."

Which meant the walkers were going to an awful lot of trouble—developing and maintaining the Agreement and this bizarre academy—just for warriors that couldn't measure up to their own kind and an occasionally useful wildcard. And they were putting kids and their families through hell to achieve it.

Theus was watching my face, trying to guess at my thoughts. "Yes. Though perhaps it would comfort you to know that the ritual is dangerous for the walkers involved too."

While I was glad to hear it wasn't *only* the humans taking the risk, it was a cold comfort when I thought of the comatose kid in the infirmary. Of Fletcher completely changed. And of how bleak my future would look if Bryn or Ameline didn't come out of the creepy chamber.

"Then why?" I asked. "Walkers already have more power than anyone should need to possess. Why do you need us? Why rip us from our families and force us through all this pain and suffering and risk for what sounds like a mediocre result?"

"And who is this enemy that has the walkers so scared?" Bryn added.

Theus's expression shut down. "I'm afraid I can't tell you that yet. You'll find out after your transformation."

I was trying to keep my frustration under control. I really was. But the absurdity of that made me want to scream.

"That makes no sense! If we're allowed to know once we complete the ritual, why can't we know now? If we die, the knowledge dies with us, and if we survive, you'll tell us then."

Theus was quiet for a long moment before he answered. And when he spoke, his tone reflected none of my anger back at me. It was aggravatingly calm.

"I have learned that when something seems to make no sense, it is often for lack of understanding rather than lack of reason."

I scowled. "And I've learned that when people refuse to give straight answers to perfectly reasonable questions, those reasons are never good!"

Theus winced.

"What aren't you telling us?" I pressed. "And why? Does the ritual change who we are? Do we become mentally enslaved to you or something?"

"No. Nothing like that."

I waited, but when he didn't elaborate, I flung up my hands in exasperation.

"Why should we believe you? I saw my old friend from a previous year. He was completely changed."

Understanding flickered in Theus's moss-green eyes. "I suppose you're too young to have seen what war does to people. One cannot be exposed to its brutality and remain the same. That was true on your planet even before the world walkers came."

He paused, then met my gaze directly.

"I don't know your friend, but it would have been the war that changed him. The ritual doesn't affect your personality, your mind, your humanity—anything that makes you who you are."

For some reason I believed him.

And my heart ached for Fletcher all over again. What horrors had he lived through to wrought such a change in him? Was it possible that some of the old Fletcher I knew remained buried deep inside?

"I have a question," Ameline said.

Theus smiled at her. "Go ahead."

"What happened to all the others? The kids on the second list. Where were they taken?"

"I can't disclose their location, but there's no need to worry on their account. They will live out their lives in relative peace."

"Uh-huh," Bryn countered. "And just how long will their supposedly peaceful lives last?"

Theus's face registered amusement at her pointed question.

"Their natural durations. Look, I know it's hard to believe after everything you've been through and all the secrecy around what was going to happen to the kids that failed. But the professors intend it to be unknown and unnerving so that no one tries to throw the results. If the truth was revealed from the start, very few, if any, would strive toward the path you're on."

I was less sure whether I believed that as well. But I hoped it was true.

Regardless, there was nothing I could do for them. Nothing more than what I was already doing, than I'd ever planned to do. To plot, scheme, and play nice until I could bring the Agreement and everything it entailed to its knees.

And to make sure Ameline and Bryn survived to see it.

So I glanced at my friends in silent question, and when they shrugged, I turned to Theus once more. "Thank you." The words sounded stiff and ungrateful, so I added, "For answering our questions."

"Most of them anyway," Bryn tacked on, voicing my own mental amendment.

Theus recognized his cue to leave. "You're welcome. I hope it allows you to be well rested before the ordeal."

He glided across the room toward me, stopping only when he was so near our breath mingled.

"Lirielle asked me to give you this."

He pressed a piece of parchment into my hand, his warm fingertips brushing mine, and let himself out.

"What is it? What does it say?" Ameline and Bryn asked. They were doubtless remembering Lirielle's cryptic but accurate warning about the stairs like I was.

With a mixture of trepidation and curiosity, I unfolded the note and scanned the single line there. Then I threw back my head and laughed.

*Take heart, Wildcard. Your magic will shake the worlds.*

# CHAPTER 32

Three months ago, we'd stepped through that runegate in complete and utter ignorance. We'd feared servitude or torment or slaughter—whatever it took to save our families. The worst of those hadn't happened, although it hadn't been too far off in some ways either.

But we'd survived.

We'd learned.

We'd become stronger.

And we would go through this transformation ritual and become stronger still.

I smiled to myself as Healer Invermoore led me down to the basement. Yes, we would continue to learn. Continue to grow and survive. And maybe, just maybe, we'd make it so that one day, no one else would have to step through a damn runegate in complete and utter ignorance again.

But I was keeping that hope to myself for now.

So I pretended not to know where Invermoore was leading me. Pretended to be surprised when the wall slid beneath Millicent's foundations. Pretended not to know what was coming.

And then I stepped voluntarily inside my creepy transformation chamber. One of many, I understood now.

I would play along. I would let the walkers gift me with the power to destroy them.

Why not?

They'd damn well regret the day they did.

Healer Invermoore touched my temple, and I slumped onto the waiting bed and let oblivion claim me.

## CHAPTER 33

Three days later, though I didn't know it at the time, my eyes opened to darkness.

And I felt effing fantastic...

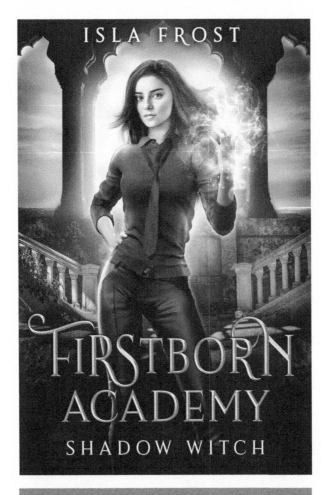

# ABOUT THE AUTHOR

Isla Frost is the pen name of a bestselling mystery author whose first love has always been fantasy. She loves to write about strong heroines in fast-paced stories full of danger, magic, and adventure that leave you feeling warm and satisfied.

She also loves apple pie.

For sneaky discounts on new releases and occasional bonus content, sign up at www.islafrost.com